I0575721

DIRTY DIGITS

by Geeta Narayan

Copyright © 2025 Geeta Narayan

All rights reserved. No part of this publication may be reproduced, distributed, or transmitted in any form or by any means, including photocopying, recording, or other electronic or mechanical methods, without the prior written permission of the publisher, except in the case of brief quotations embodied in critical reviews and certain other noncommercial uses permitted by copyright law.

In Loving Memory of

Terence Vishal Mishra

You Are Missed Every Day

Dedicated to my son,

Rahul Brennan Narayan

This book is a heartfelt tribute: to the indomitable Fijian spirit, to lovers who blossom amidst adversity, and to the unwavering resolve of those pursuing atonement. Suva's essence pulsates within these pages potent, visceral narrative woven from the sights, sounds, and aromas of the island. A captivating rhythm pulsed through the air, the *meke*—a traditional Fijian dance—hypnotizing all who witnessed it. Dancers, a vibrant blur of *masi* (bark cloth), moved with ethereal grace, their bodies becoming vessels for the mystical fusion of earthly and spiritual energies. The sharp, earthy tang of *yaqona* (also known as kava, root of the piper methysticum plant), a potent brew shared with unshakeable devotion, is exquisitely counterbalanced by the delicate sweetness of frangipani, its intoxicating fragrance, a fragrant balm against the kava's bitterness.

Suva throbs with unrestrained joy, a dazzling contrast to the low, resonant chants murmuring from hidden corners. These age-old, powerful whispers narrate sagas of resilience and unwavering fortitude, of gods and spectral entities. The city is a stunning mosaic of contradictions, a fiercely beating, untamed heart. It's a haven for the indomitable, those who have triumphed over hardship, finding comfort in the bonds of empathetic camaraderie. It shelters the dreamers, those who bravely stake their futures on their aspirations; the passionately devoted; and the flawed yet inherently good souls who meet life's complex trials and the tangled mysteries of love with indomitable spirit.

And especially...for those who dare to dream of a better tomorrow, even after facing the sting of past failures. This is for those who choose love and loyalty despite the odds. This is for the people of Suva; their resilience, their generosity, their spirit inspired by these words. May this story be a testament to the transformative power of second chances, unwavering dedication, and the enduring strength of the human spirit, against any odds.

Table of Contents

Preface

This narrative springs from a deep-seated preoccupation with humanity's deep-rooted contradictions. We possess an extraordinary capacity for boundless affection yet remain tragically susceptible to grievous errors. Haunted by a shadowy past, Day Marshall, a master of deceit and expert thief, is a man of profound contradictions: a brilliant lock-picker consumed by his remorse, yet incandescently loyal to the woman who holds his heart captive.

His journey is one of self-destruction and redemption, mirroring the internal battles many faces when grappling with their past. Writing this story allowed me to explore the intricacies of a relationship tested by crime, imprisonment, and refreshing *my own* cultural complexities of the Fijian society. My birthplace, Suva, a city pulsating with life, indelibly shaped my early years. I vividly recall its teeming markets and shadowy cafes, a heady mix of scents: the savory perfume of freshly cooked *roti* and the sizzling allure of *fish and chips*. The sweetness of *milkshake* and *lamington* parlors, the riotous profusion of *hibiscus* and *bougainvillea*, stood in stark, unsettling comparison to the city's grimmer, criminal reality—a potent and unforgettable setting for this story. The story's profound authenticity stems from the meticulous study of Fijian society and its complex legal framework, immersing the reader in a world at once recognizable and breathtakingly unique. The research extended beyond the purely factual, exploring the emotional heart of the Fijian people, their strength and

i

resilience and the deep cultural bonds that *we* weave together as a society. The hope is to have created a world that is both compelling and respectful of the rich heritage of Fiji. It is my hope that this story resonates with readers, not only for its romantic and criminal elements, but also for its portrayal of resilience, love, and the possibility of redemption.

Introduction

This is a story of love and crime, set against the vibrant backdrop of Suva, Fiji. Day Marshall's extraordinary skill at cracking safes was his curse and his calling, an uncertain duality that defined his life. His life is a dangerously delicate dance between exhilarating risk and devastating consequences. His love for Adelyn, a dedicated nurse, is the anchor that tethers him to a life beyond the shadowy world of criminal enterprise.

Their bond is a tempestuous voyage, marked by ecstatic peaks and agonizing troughs. Day's repeated incarcerations relentlessly strain their devotion, plunging them into a vortex of emotional turmoil. A fiery passion burns between them, visible in the adoring gazes they exchange, eyes brimming with affection and yearning. Yet, each confinement casts a shadow of profound sorrow across their faces, a stark testament to their enduring struggle. Undeterred, however, they cling to each other, navigating the treacherous currents of their love. Adelyn's unwavering love, punctuated by bouts of heartbreaking frustration, forms the emotional core of this narrative.

The story unfolds within the familiar confines of their community – the bustling Roti Shop where Day lives above in a one-bedroom apartment, the sterile environment of *CWM hospital* (Colonial War Memorial Hospital) where Adelyn works, and the shadowy corners where Day plies his illicit trade. We are introduced to the enigmatic Maddaar, a figure whose cryptic pronouncements add a layer of mystery and suspense to the plot. Their interactions shape Day's destiny and illuminate a hidden side of Fijian society, adding richness and texture to the storyline.

This is a story about the choices we make, the consequences we face, and the transformative power of unwavering love. It is a journey into the heart of a man wrestling with his demons, a woman struggling to reconcile her love with her despair, and a community grappling with the complexities of life and love in a world that isn't always black and white. Prepare yourself for a story that will challenge your assumptions, ignite your emotions, and leave you breathless until the very last page.

First Meeting in the Roti Shop's Glow

Suva's core pulsed with the intoxicating fragrance of the Roti Shop; a rich, almost overpowering sweetness, a captivating blend of turmeric, ginger, and fiercely sputtering oil saturated the air. This alluring perfume, a persistent memory, clung stubbornly to the senses, leaving an enduring olfactory impression long after one had left. Sandwiched between the bustling Suva Market and the Harbour Centre, a vestige of colonial design now sheltered a chaotic collection of tiny businesses and dwellings. The Suva Wharf offered a breathtaking panorama from the shop's doorway. The vibrant colors of hibiscus, bougainvillea, and frangipani, blooming along the meandering waterway that snaked through the city, the frenetic activity of Suva Market, and the invigorating saltiness of the sea air coalesced into a truly unforgettable sensory experience.

A subtle quiver betrayed the anxiety etched onto his face, a captivating mosaic of Fijian and English heritage. Perched unsteadily on the rickety stool, his noble features formed a striking, indefinable features. A breathtaking joining of ancestral lineages, his appearance was a stunning spectacle of rare beauty, powerfully highlighting the artistry of mixed ancestry. A strong, chiseled jawline supported a face of arresting handsomeness. His hair, a captivating wave of texture, shimmered with highlights the color of sunset amber. From beneath his brow, smoldering, dark eyes burned with an intense, captivating light. Dressed in loose, khaki trousers

1

and a summery blue linen shirt, splashed with bold tropical blooms and casual flip flops, he had an aura of enigmatic charm, a silent promise of untold stories.

A lukewarm beer sat sluggishly in his hand, each sip measured, deliberate. His gaze, seemingly casual, drifted across the room, yet beneath the surface, a sharp, hawk-like attention preyed on the scene. Etched onto his lean frame was the brutal history of a life balanced precariously on the razor's edge. He was a man sculpted by hardship, his wiry muscles a testament to countless battles with fate. A volatile energy crackled in his eyes; the threat of swift, brutal violence hung heavy in the atmosphere. Day Marshall commanded attention.

From across the crowded room, his gaze was instantly drawn to her. A captivating paradox, she embodied a stunning contrast: the pristine, almost severe lines of her white nurse's uniform clashed dramatically with the vibrant chaos of the Roti Shop. Her pristine outfit, a stark testament to controlled precision, radiated an almost ethereal light. Her sleek, raven Indian hair, tightly bound in a chignon, masked a fiery soul. A few rebellious strands softened the haunting beauty and quiet sorrow on her striking features. Later, her name, Adelyn Nath, was whispered between them, bonding them in secretive intimacy. Her eyes, the bottomless hue of a tranquil, deep sea, held a mesmerizing depth that captivated Day. They mirrored both an inner fortitude and a subtle sadness that

resonated profoundly within him. His eyes lingered on her slender legs, the rich, delectable shade of smooth milk chocolate. She sat solitary, engrossed in a half-eaten roti meal, seemingly unaware of the Roti Shop's frenetic energy, a serene island in a turbulent sea.

Day Marshall, a master of his craft, could pick locks with ease, but he found his hands trembling as he imagined himself approaching her. He knew about these places, these islands of refuge in the sea of uncertainty that were the roti shops and cafes. The comforting familiarity, the shared stories, and the aroma of the spiced food held people together. And somehow, amid all the chaos controlled, he sensed that he should approach this island of peace. He wasn't usually so hesitant.

He watched her for a moment longer, captivated by the subtle movement of her lips as she spoke quietly to herself, a soft murmur that seemed to be more prayer than conversation. He saw a flicker of sadness cross her features, a melancholic trace that mirrored his own inner turmoil. He knew that darkness, that shadow that hung around him. He could see it reflected in her eyes.

Then, as if driven by an unseen force, he rose from his stool. The beer, half-empty and lukewarm, felt heavy in his hand. Each step felt monumental, every footstep a thunderous beat against the rhythmic clatter of the kitchen. He moved through the crowded space, the air thick with the spicy scent of curry, the murmur of conversations creating a hypnotic hum, pulling him towards her as though bound by an invisible thread.

His arrival was a palpable shift; the room's frenetic energy subsided, yielding to the weight of his deliberate progress toward her. A hush, thick with unspoken longing, descended. He could feel the gazes of the other patrons shift to him, a silent audience witnessing the unfolding of a new story. He arrived at her table and paused, a fleeting moment of hesitation before he spoke. His voice, rough from years of smoking and late nights, was surprisingly gentle.

"*Bula* (hello) mind if I sit?" he asked, his gaze meeting hers with an intensity that seemed to bridge the distance between them. Adelyn looked up, startled but not unfriendly. Her eyes, those deep ocean pools, held a trace of surprise, but there was no fear, only a quiet curiosity. She nodded, a small, almost unnoticeable movement of her head. Day slid onto the stool opposite her, the squeak of the metal a jarring interruption to the comfortable silence that had settled between them.

"I'm Day," he said, extending a hand callused from years of hard work or perhaps something else entirely.

"Adelyn," she responded, her small and soft hand in his, a gentle touch that sent a jolt of unexpected warmth through him. Her touch was a stark contrast to his rough exterior. The moment stretched, their hands clasped for what seemed like eternity, a silent communication passing between them, a mutual understanding that transcended words.

The conversation that followed was a meandering stream, starting with the usual pleasantries about the weather and the quality of the roti, then veering off into unexpected directions, like a winding Fijian river. They talked about their lives, their dreams, their fears. Adelyn spoke of her work at CWM Hospital, the long hours, the emotional toll, the small moments of kindness that made the job worthwhile. Day, guarded at first, began to open, sharing fragments of his life, carefully omitting certain details, yet revealing enough to pique her interest.

He mentioned his skills, a veiled reference to his abilities that hinted at life beyond the Roti Shop's humble confines. Adelyn listened intently, her eyes shining with a mixture of curiosity and apprehension. She sensed something about him that was both alluring and dangerous, a wildness that contrasted sharply with her own careful, controlled existence.

As the hours passed, the Roti Shop gradually emptied, the vibrant energy of the earlier evening fading into a quiet hum. They remained seated at their table, lost in their own world, the aroma of spices and the gentle murmur of conversations creating a tapestry of intimacy around them. The glow of the shop's lights seemed to enhance the beauty of Adelyn's face, the light highlighting the delicate curve of her cheekbones and the warm hue of her skin. The shadows that played around Day's face seemed to soften, revealing a hint of vulnerability that hadn't been apparent before.

Outside, the sounds of Suva were toned down, the night offering a hushed break from the day's clamor. Inside, the warmth of the Roti Shop and the rapidly growing connection between Day and Adelyn created a haven of their own. Their first meeting, a chance encounter in the bustling heart of Suva, was a spark, a flicker of something powerful and profound that neither of them could quite comprehend, but both desperately wanted to explore. It was the beginning, the genesis of a relationship that would be marked by passion, danger, and ultimately, a profound and transformative sacrifice. The seeds of their complex tale were sown in that small, dimly lit Roti

Shop, amongst the fragrant spices and the warm, comforting glow of the lights. The scent of curry and the taste of roti would forever be intertwined with their memories of this pivotal first meeting. They finished their rotis, curry and beers as the first hint of dawn crept in through the windows.

The lingering aroma of ginger and cardamom filled the air as Day walked Adelyn back towards her home, the rhythmic sounds of the night a tranquil background to their brand-new connection. The silence between them was not uncomfortable but rather a space filled with unspoken questions and unspoken promises, a space that hummed with the electric current of mutual attraction. The warmth of the Roti Shop's glow still seemed to linger, wrapping them in a comfortable cocoon as they navigated the shadowy streets of upper Suva together. The future, with its inherent uncertainty, beckoned before them, a landscape yet to be explored, a journey yet to be undertaken, hand in hand, their stories entwined.

The next few years *would* prove how strong or how weak that initial connection truly was. It would test the strength of a love born under the warm, inviting glow of a simple Suva Roti Shop. The air hung thick and sweet, a heady blend of chilies, ginger, and frying onions clinging to the worn wooden beams of Papa Ram and Mama Sita's intimate Roti Shop.

Day's Criminal Underbelly Revealed

Papa Ram, his apron, a canvas splashed with turmeric and chili stains, shimmered as he moved. A glint of mischief, not quite a twinkle, danced in his eyes as he plucked a fat green chili, its stem still clinging stubbornly, and, with a flick of his wrist, minced it into a vibrant paste. Flour dusted his forearms, a testament to hours spent kneading dough – a mountain of it, pale and yielding, rising slowly beside a bubbling pot of lentils, their earthy scent intertwining with the sharp bite of the chili. He hummed an old *Bollywood* tune, a rhythm that mirrored the steady slap of his hands on the dough. "*Bula* (hello, how are you) sweetheart" He murmured, a deep baritone barely audible, "Care for a refill, my dear?" His hand, swift and sure, already grasped the flask brimming with steaming, cocoa-rich warmth.

His wife, Mama Sita, a short slender woman with an unforgettable smile that could thaw even the coldest of glaciers, welcomed customers with a gentle poise that reflected their unwavering warmth. Her presence filled the air with a sweet fragrance of hospitality, evoking a sense of comfort and familiarity. Mama Sita's charming smile lingered long after she said her warm greetings, leaving customers with a sense of belonging. Her innate grace and hospitality were noticeable in the air, making every visit a memorable experience.

The clinking of glasses and the low hum of conversation faded into the background as Adelyn leaned closer, her breath warm against Day's ear. "You haven't told me much about your work, Day," she whispered, her voice barely audible above the rhythmic clatter of cutlery. He shifted uncomfortably; the casual ease he'd cultivated earlier dissolving into a tense stillness. The playful banter of the Roti Shop felt miles away, replaced by a sudden, stark awareness of the chasm that separated their worlds.

He took a long swallow of his beer, the cold liquid a stark contrast to the warmth spreading through his chest. He'd always been careful, keeping the details of his profession vague, a carefully constructed wall between his carefully curated public persona and the reality of his life. "It's...complicated," he mumbled, avoiding her gaze. The simple phrase hung in the air, heavy with unspoken implications.

Adelyn's hand found his, her touch gentle yet insistent. "Tell me", She urged softly, her eyes reflecting the soft glow of the Roti Shop's lights. He felt a pang of guilt, a familiar ache in his chest. He knew he couldn't keep deceiving her forever. But the truth, the messy, dangerous truth of his existence, felt like a viper coiled in his heart, ready to strike. He loved her desperately, fiercely, but the life he led threatened to consume them both.

A shard of memory surfaced: the chilling metallic bite of a padlock, the precise pressure of his fingers, and the satisfying click as the mechanism yielded. It was a dance, a silent conversation between him and the inanimate object, a test of skill and patience. He was good, damn good, at what he did. Too good, perhaps. The ease with which he could slip into shadows, navigate the underbelly of Suva's nightlife, the thrill of the risk, it was an addiction as potent as any drug. He haunted the city's underbelly, a phantom leaving a trail of devastation in his wake.

His brutality found a grotesque embodiment in the frail woman of Marks Street. The callous raid of her heirloom jewels demolished her once-peaceful existence, transforming her into a sorrowful, spectral testament to his corruptness. His destructive acts left a grim, enduring stain on the city's underworld, a mournful *dirge* for his victims. The price, however, was staggering. A paralyzing fear, a relentless shadow, haunted him, the ever-present risk of prosecution a suffocating weight on his soul.

He vividly recalled the night the police swarmed his apartment, their harsh voices echoing in the cramped space, the fluorescent lights blinding him as they meticulously searched, leaving him trembling, a prisoner in his own home, the chilling certainty of potential imprisonment settling heavily on his soul – a visceral memory that indelibly marked him, a constant reminder of the price he had paid.

Months after Suva's Remand Center, the stench of despair –a clinging shroud – still clung to him. The prison hadn't just scarred his soul; it had burrowed into his very being. The air, a fetid pall of hopelessness and madness, stole his self-respect and faith. The bitter taste of despair lingered, metallic like blood. Haunted by the grotesque faces – hollowed eyes reflecting extinguished humanity – he saw old Manu, broken and vacant. Manu's whispered pleas for solace echoed in his ears, a stark contrast to the guards' brutal sneers: "Worthless." This condemnation crushed him. Yet, his face shone brighter

– a defiant young man, his spirit a flickering flame amidst the grime. This resilience both terrified and captivated him. The Remand Centre's echoing corridors, the clang of steel, and the pervasive stench of fear were a symphony of terror, a festering wound, a constant reminder of his vulnerability. The screams still echoed – a deafening chorus in his heart. A part of him remained trapped, forever stained by the darkness. Those memories haunted him, dark specters lurking in the shadows of his mind. He never talked about those experiences, not even with Adelyn, the image of the cold, damp cells and the stench of despair too grim for words. The faces swam in his mind, a rogues' gallery etched in the grime of his soul.

Tevita – that wiry viper, his breath a cocktail of cheap gin and city secrets. The man smelled of shadowed alleyways and desperation, the reek clinging to him like a second skin. His network pulsed beneath the city, a throbbing vein of whispered deals and broken promises, each connection a flicker of danger in the smoky, opium-tinged air of Suva's dens. He could practically taste the fear on Tevita's tongue, a bitter tang mixing with the sweetness of his illicit gains.

And then there was Moji – an Asian predator draped in silk, all feline grace and calculated charm. The chill of her touch lingered, a memory as sharp as broken glass. Her fingers, long and elegant, managed the spoils of Day's bloody endeavors with a surgeon's precision, each transaction a dance of risk and reward. The scent of expensive perfume couldn't mask the metallic tang of blood money clinging to her, subtle perfume of power and ruthlessness. He felt a shudder – a visceral revulsion battling a desperate fascination. They were his shadows, these people, and he was inextricably bound to their

10

darkness. And then there was the enigmatic Maddaar, a recluse who lived on the fringes of society, a man shrouded in mystery, his past a tangled web of rumours and whispers.

These were the people who inhabited the city's underbelly, a world hidden beneath the veneer of vibrant tourism and bustling markets. A world of stolen goods, hushed transactions, and coded messages. Day was a part of that world, a skilled player in a dangerous game, but he felt trapped, entangled in a web of his own making. He yearned for something different, something cleaner, something…normal. He wanted a life where his skills weren't used to violate trust, where his nimble fingers didn't unlock doors that shouldn't be opened. He wanted a life with Adelyn, a life where he wasn't constantly looking over his shoulder, where he wasn't haunted by the ghosts of his past. Adelyn squeezed his hand, breaking through his reverie. "Day," she said softly, her voice laced with concern, "I know something's bothering you. You can tell me." Her honesty, her unwavering trust, it was a fragile thing, a precious bloom that could be easily crushed. He knew he was pushing her to her limits, assessing the boundaries of her patience. But he wasn't sure he had the strength to change, to pull himself free from the grip of the criminal underworld. He had made his choices, and now he was paying the price.

The rhythmic sounds of the night seemed to intensify as he walked her home – the distant rumble of a vehicle, the occasional bark of a dog, and the murmur of voices from the nearby houses. Each sound felt like a hammer blow against the fragile wall he had built around his secrets. The vibrant, bustling energy of the Roti Shop was replaced with a heavier silence, the air thick with unspoken anxieties.

He saw a flash of a memory – a panicked call in the dead of night, a frantic search for a specific tool, the frantic rush to a high-security building, the thrilling adrenaline rush that came with a successful heist, the bitter taste of victory and the lingering dread of what could follow. The thought of Adelyn's disapproval, the potential fracture in their flourishing relationship sent another wave of guilt crashing over him.

He thought about the risks. The possibility of a botched job, the potential for violence, the long-term consequences of a life lived in the shadows. He'd seen men disappear without a trace, their lives vanishing into the city's unforgiving depths. He knew the police were always a step behind, often just out of reach, but he knew they were watching, always watching.

The weight of the life he led, the ever-present threat of discovery, weighed heavily on his mind. He knew that Adelyn deserved better, a life free from the constant fear and uncertainty that shadowed his existence. But the allure of the game, the adrenaline rush, the thrill of the chase, it was something he struggled to break free from. It was a part of him, a dark side he couldn't simply erase. He was a product of his environment, molded by the harsh realities of his upbringing, a skilled safecracker who'd never known anything else.

He tried to speak, to explain, but the words caught in his throat. The words seemed inadequate, hollow in the face of his complicated truth. The weight of his past, the shadows that clung to him, seemed impossible to overcome. He closed his eyes, letting out a long, shaky breath. The future, once a bright, hopeful prospect, now seemed uncertain, shrouded in the gray mists of doubt and fear. The love he felt for Adelyn was a beacon, a guiding light in the darkness, but he wasn't sure if he could ever escape the shadows that clung to him, the shadows that defined his life. His past was a dangerous, unpredictable beast, and it was slowly but surely destroying everything he held dear.

Adelyn's Compassion and Dilemma

The silence stretched thick and heavy between them, punctuated only by the distant clatter of plates and the murmur of voices from the Roti Shop below. Adelyn's gaze drifted to the flickering neon sign outside, its light painting fleeting shadows on Day's face, highlighting the tension etched around his eyes. She saw the weariness, the burden he carried, a weight heavier than any *safe* he'd ever cracked. He was an expert in deception, a phantom in the Suva night, yet with her, he was vulnerable, exposed, a man wrestling with a darkness he could not seem to outrun.

The glacial fragment, a shard of agonizing cold, transfixed Adelyn, a perfect reflection of the desolate void consuming her. His neglected lily plant, a pathetic monument to their deceased affection, choked her spirit, every inhalation a torment. The ferocious intensity of her love, a ravenous predator, had devoured her, leaving only a hollow shell.

Adelyn's fingers traced the rim of her glass, the condensation chilling her skin. CWM Hospital, a sterile arena of hushed prayers and stifled sobs, was a stark contrast to Day's suffocating world of deceit. The hospital air, heavy with lilies and blood, pulsed with raw energy, life's fragility, a gasping breath, a heart monitor's countdown. Weary families' love flickered against illness's encroaching darkness. Fear clung to the dying; dignity surrendered to mortality. Honesty, a lifeline in the chaos, was absent from Day's fetid Suva, a swamp of

14

treachery where trust was venomous. Yesterday, a terrified mother clutched a wilted hibiscus, whispering to her feverish child. Their desperate hope, mirrored in their eyes, was a fragile hibiscus bloom, easily crushed by Day's world – a world trading hope for dollars, where lilies yielded to corruption, sterile white to suffocating darkness. The chasm between our realities – a terrifying abyss – remains.

She understood his skill, his almost supernatural ability to manipulate locks and bypass security systems. She'd seen the meticulous planning, the cool precision, the almost artistic flair with which he operated. It was a talent, a gift, she couldn't deny, but one that fueled his dangerous path. The irony wasn't lost on her: he possessed the delicate touch of a surgeon yet wielded it for nefarious purposes. He could unlock a heart as easily as he could unlock a safe, but the hearts he touched often ended up broken, including her own. The weight of his secrets pressed down on her, a suffocating burden. He'd never explicitly admitted his involvement in criminal activities, yet his disappearances, his evasiveness, and his sudden bursts of wealth spoke volumes. She'd seen the lingering bruises on his arms, the subtle limp that suggested a recent confrontation. The stories whispered in the hushed tones of the Roti Shop, the sideways glances from familiar faces, all painted a picture far more sinister than anything he'd ever confessed.

The aroma of roti and curry, usually a source of comfort, did little to ease the tension. The lively chatter of the other patrons seemed distant, muted, as if a soundproof wall had separated them from the rest of the world. Adelyn felt a knot of anxiety tighten in her stomach.

She offered *the book,* it's leather cool against her trembling fingers, a silent offering against the cacophony of hate. The rough texture of the pages, the faint scent of old paper and forgotten stories – it was a lifeline thrown into the maelstrom. She saw it reflected in his haunted eyes – the bleak landscape of his soul, a wasteland ravaged by violence. But beneath the scars, a flicker of something else, something akin to embers in the ash, ignited a fierce empathy in her. It wasn't pity; it was a terrifyingly intimate understanding, a shared burden of pain so profound it transcended words. Her response wasn't a judgment, a lecture, but a whisper of hope against the howling wind of his fury. She didn't offer redemption; she offered a weapon, a path to forge his anger into something potent, something. magnificent. It was a perilous bridge, built on the shaky foundations of compassion, balanced precariously on the razor's edge of hope – a gamble against the darkness that had claimed him, a fight for a future where the monster within might finally, miraculously become something else entirely cycle of fear and heartbreak.

She recalled a recent incident at the hospital. A young boy, barely ten years old, brought in after a brutal mugging. The boy, his face smeared with blood, his eyes filled with terror, mirrored the fear she sometimes saw in Day's eyes the same fear of vulnerability and exposure. The image haunted her, a stark reminder of the consequences of Day's actions, the ripple effect of his choices on the lives of others.

Adelyn craved a future: a sunlit farmhouse, a haven from the city's darkness and her lover's shadow. She envisioned laughter, warmth, and hand-thrown pottery – a life built on love, not fear. Yet, the phantom scent of blood constantly invaded her idyllic fantasy, a stark reminder of the brutal reality. The choice – his or her soul – was a relentless torment. His charm was captivating, her love all-consuming, but the price of happiness might be her life. In the quiet Roti Shop, the question echoed: could their love survive his darkness? Could they bridge their disparate worlds? Their future, a precarious dance between hope and despair, remained uncertain; the spices' sweetness was a cruel mask for the bitter truth – their story was far from concluded.

The air hung heavy with the unspoken words between Day and Adelyn, a silence thicker than the humid Suva night. The scent of roti, usually comforting, now felt suffocating, stark contrast to the cool breeze that occasionally drifted in through the open window of their cramped apartment above the bustling Roti Shop. Then, a shadow detached itself from the darkness of the alleyway below. A figure, tall and gaunt, appeared, silhouetted against the neon glow of the Roti Shop's sign. It was Maddaar.

Maddaar's Enigmatic Presence

A phantom of the alley, Maddaar reeked of woodsmoke and *decay*. His absences were calculated disappearances, leaving only a chilling emptiness. Predatory grace masked his immense power, his weariness, the burden of countless battles. A wide-brimmed hat concealed much of his countenance; the shadowed face partially obscured by a cloth mask. His eyes, pools of blackest obsidian, mirrored not the external world, but a profound and unsettling interiority.

A *rumor,* insidious and chilling, slithered through the city: Maddaar, supposedly perished and was laid to rest in Suva's mournful cemetery, had escaped the clutches of death. Forty-eight hours after his burial, he re-emerged into the city's cacophony, a ghastly spectacle of survival. His features, partially concealed by a cloth mask, bore the horrific signature of subterranean torment; a ravaged, mutilated nose, testament to the ravenous insects that had *feasted* upon him in his grave's icy embrace.

Day, momentarily distracted from his internal turmoil, watched Maddaar's approach with a flicker of something akin to recognition or perhaps apprehension. There was a shared history between them, unspoken yet palpable, a connection forged in the crucible of Suva's underbelly, a bond woven from shared secrets and a mutual understanding of the city's darker currents. It was a connection that Day neither acknowledged nor denied, a silent pact sealed in the shadows.

Maddaar, a phantom of the city's underbelly, clung to the buses, his scent a foul blend of diesel and sweat. A silent, brooding figure, *he rode free*, unnoticed amidst the throng. His perpetual bowed head hinted at an unseen burden. The city's noise was a dull roar around his silent passage; he was the last to leave, a shadow dissolving into the grime. Day, a man of meticulous routine, found Maddaar's spectral presence deeply unsettling. A chill, deeper than the bus's recycled air emanated from Maddaar's withdrawn form. Was he a criminal or something far stranger? His unspoken story weighed heavily on Day, a terrifying reminder that secrets are best left undisturbed, own the power to unleash the deepest fears.

Maddaar paused at the bottom of their apartment stairs. His hat-shadowed eyes, sharp and searching, seemed to bore into the night, seeking Day. A strange, wordless gesture—neither greeting nor goodbye—hung between them. Then, silently, he vanished, leaving Day alone with the lingering chill of his presence. What was that? Who was he looking for? Day thought, a prickle of unease crawling up his spine. That feeling… like something momentous is about to happen, but I don't know what. The night felt heavier now, pregnant with unspoken dread. The silence after his departure was deafening, amplifying the unanswered questions.

As dusk descended, a scrawny local newspaper lad, Shah, stumbled upon him; a solitary candle, its flame a frail dance, illuminated the timeworn pages of his treasured book. The boy, awestruck, barely audible his query: "Legend speaks of your boundless knowledge." Maddaar's hand, bearing the etched map of past trauma, gleamed faintly. His response, a rasping growl from the depths of his being, was stark: "Certain truths

19

are best left undisturbed. Others…resurface." He closed his book, its pages whispering like dried leaves. "The deadliest weapons are silent, the most potent poisons sweet," he warned. His gaze, icy and sharp, pierced Shah. "Sometimes," he murmured, "the woodsmoke scent intensifying with a metallic tang, escape lies only through deepest darkness." He returned to his book, leaving Shah shaken, the air heavy with unspoken tragedy and the chilling scent of woodsmoke and blood. He carried himself with a quiet dignity, a subtle air of authority that belied his tattered clothes and unkempt appearance. He was a riddle wrapped in an enigma, a ghost haunting the edges of their lives.

Adelyn watched Day's face, searching for any clue to the meaning of this cryptic visit. The lines around his eyes seemed to deepen, and his jaw clenched tighter. He was brooding, lost in the labyrinth of his own thoughts. "Who was that?" Adelyn finally asked, her voice barely a whisper, as if afraid to break the fragile silence that had settled over them once more. Day didn't answer immediately. He took a long drag from his cigarette, the ember glowing like a tiny, defiant star in the darkness. The smoke curled upwards, momentarily obscuring his face, before dissipating into the night. When he spoke, his voice was low, almost a murmur, "Just Maddaar."

"Maddaar?" Adelyn repeated, the name sounding strangely alien on her tongue. She had heard whispers about him, tales told in hushed tones in the Roti Shop, stories of a man who had vanished and returned, a man with a past as murky and unpredictable as the Suva harbor at night. Day remained silent, his gaze fixed on a distant point beyond the window, a faraway look in his eyes. The silence stretched between them, filled only with the faint hum of the city, a low, persistent drone that seemed to mirror the unspoken tension between them. He seemed distant, lost in a world Adelyn couldn't access, a world of shadows and secrets that were both alluring and terrifying.

Adelyn understood then that Maddaar was more than just a mysterious figure in their neighborhood. He was a symbol, a tangible representation of the hidden currents that shaped Day's life, the undertow that pulled him relentlessly toward the darkness. He stood for the choices Day had made, the path he had chosen to walk, and the consequences that inevitably followed. In their apartment, Adelyn rose and walked to the window, pushing aside the flimsy curtain. The city lights shimmered in the distance, a glittering tapestry woven from hope and despair, promise and betrayal. Suva was a city of star contrasts, a place where paradise and peril danced in a dangerous tango. The vibrant culture, the lush tropical landscapes, the warmth of its people – all coexisted uneasily with the pervasive poverty, the simmering unrest, and the ever-present threat of violence. It was a city that mirrored Day himself: a man of immense talent and charm, capable of great kindness and devastating cruelty. He was a master of disguise, able to blend. Seamlessly into any environment, yet his heart remained as exposed and vulnerable as a freshly plucked hibiscus.

The thought of Day's dual existence, his ability to slip so effortlessly between his two worlds, struck Adelyn with a fresh wave of sadness. She longed for him to embrace fully the life they could have together, a life free from the shadow of his past, a future where love could finally conquer all. But the visit from Maddaar, that enigmatic, fleeting apparition, had only served to deepen her anxieties. It was a stark reminder of the complex web of relationships, the invisible threads of connection, which bound them all together, creating a tapestry of secrets and shared destinies in the heart of Suva.

Days passed in a blur of anxiety and anticipation. Day remained strangely subdued; his usual boisterous energy replaced by a quiet intensity. He spent hours staring out of the window, lost in contemplation, while Adelyn struggled to reconcile her love for him with the ever-present threat of his criminal activities.

One evening, as they sat in their small apartment, the aroma of roti mingling with the scent of cumin and cloves from Adelyn's cooking, the conversation turned back to Maddaar. This time, Day spoke willingly, though with a palpable reluctance. "He… he knows things," Day began, his voice raspy from disuse. He paused, taking a long drag from his cigarette, the smoke obscuring his eyes again. "Things about me… things about us." Adelyn's heart pounded in her chest. The air grew thick with unspoken words, heavy with the weight of the mystery that surrounded Maddaar, and the subtle hints of danger that clung to Day like a shadow. "What things?" Adelyn whispered, her voice barely audible above the hum of the city. Fear gnawed at her, a cold dread that gripped her insides. Day looked at her, his eyes filled with a mixture of guilt and resignation. "Things that could ruin us," he said simply, his voice laced with a weariness that spoke volumes. "Things better left buried." He didn't elaborate, but the implications hung in the air, a suffocating weight that pressed down on them both.

Maddaar's enigmatic presence, his fleeting appearance, and Day's cryptic statements had woven a thread of suspense into their lives, adding a layer of complexity and uncertainty to their already turbulent relationship. The future, once uncertain, now felt shrouded in a veil of secrecy, a dangerous game of cat and mouse with an unseen adversary.

The aroma of the night blooming jasmine now served as a constant reminder of their precarious existence, of their fragile love hanging in the balance, a testament to the fragile nature of happiness in a city steeped in both beauty and brutality. The shadow of Maddaar's presence seemed to loom over them, a constant reminder of the secrets they held and the risks they were willing to take for their love, a love that might, just might, prove strong enough to weather the storm. The question lingered: Could their love survive the darkness that clung to Day like a shadow, or would the enigmatic Maddaar and the secrets he held ultimately tear them apart? The answer remained elusive, a mystery to be unravelled in the heart of Suva. The city, a breathtaking backdrop of paradise and peril, awaited the next chapter in their story, a story where love and crime danced a delicate and dangerous waltz.

The First Arrest and its Aftermath

The taste of stale sweat, and fear still clung to Day's throat, an illusionary echo of the vault's suffocating darkness. He had felt the ancient stone cold against his cheek, the sickeningly sweet tang of ozone as the laser sliced through the steel. The rhythmic thump-thump-thump of his own heart, a frantic drum solo against the silence, had been the only sound louder than the agonizingly slow grind of the tumblers yielding to his ability. A phantom, he had moved unseen through the nocturnal gloom, leaving behind only a ravaged repository at the vibrant Cumming Street Westpac Bank, a seemingly commonplace hub of ceaseless financial activity and the echoing aftermath of his daring robbery. The chilling weight of his crime, a devastating torrent of consequences, relentlessly pursued him.

Then, the pre-dawn quiet – the fragile, paper-thin quiet of a sleeping city –exploded. Not a shattering, but a rupture. The raw, guttural roar of the police jeep's engine ripped through the stillness, a metallic beast awakening from its slumber. It's headlights, twin cyclopean eyes, sliced through the darkness, bathing the street in an icy, accusing glare. The air seemed to vibrate with the approaching menace; Day could feel the tremor in his boots, the metallic tang of exhaust fumes stinging his nostrils, the coarse gravel spitting against his ankles as the jeep screeched to a halt a breath away from his window. The jarring crash of the vehicle's sudden stop was punctuated by the sickening *thunk* of its door slamming shut – a sound that echoed the finality of his freedom ending. Panic, cold and sharp as shattered glass, clawed at his gut. The game was over.

A blinding flash seared Adelyn awake, a metallic taste of terror coating her tongue. The usual flimsy curtains offered no shield against the invasive, pulsing beam, which contorted the shadows into grotesque shapes. The familiar smell of burning spices from below now felt suffocating, a stark contrast to the icy fear gripping her. Her heart pounded a frantic rhythm, mirroring the adrenaline surge. This wasn't a flashlight; it was a predator's stare, shattering her sense of security. Day was gone. A bone-chilling dread seized her; something was horribly wrong.

She scrambled out of bed, her nightgown twisting around her legs, and rushed to the window. Below, in the weak, orange glow of the streetlights, she saw him. Day, his hands cuffed behind his back, was being shoved roughly into the back of the jeep. His face, usually alight with a mischievous glint, was pale and drawn, etched with a mixture of defiance and resignation. He caught her eye for a fleeting moment, a silent plea, a desperate attempt to convey something, anything, across the chasm that was suddenly opening between them. But the jeep doors slammed shut, swallowing him whole.

The scent of antiseptic and despair clung to her. The comforting rhythm of the Roti Shop and the familiar chaos of Suva's early morning bustle all faded into a blurry, indistinct background. All that remained was the gaping hole left by Day's absence, a void that echoed with the deafening silence of his loss. She stumbled back, clutching the windowsill, her body trembling with a mixture of shock and grief.

Adelyn's world shattered. A vision of cracks mirrored the pain in her chest. The precinct air – fear and stale coffee –tasted like ash. Each footstep echoed like a gunshot, a rhythm against her frantic heart. Pacing, she felt caged, her fingers digging into her coat. "Did you check the security footage? Frame by frame?" Her melodic voice was a rasping accusation. The officer's silence confirmed her worst fears. Sweat prickled her skin; a chill gripped her. She slammed her fist on the table. "He wouldn't…" The unfinished sentence, heavy with unspoken horror, hung in the air. Tears blurred her vision. She questioned reality itself; her life lay in ruins, a wreckage she faced alone.

The following days were a blur. Adelyn navigated the labyrinthine corridors of Suva's Central Police Station, a stark contrast to the sterile, controlled environment of CWM Hospital. The air here hung heavy with despair, a potent cocktail of stale cigarette smoke, sweat, and the lingering scent of fear. Each encounter with a uniformed officer, each exchange of clipped words and official documents, was a painful reminder of Day's predicament. The first shock gave way to a gnawing anxiety, a relentless tide of worry that threatened to consume her. Sleep became a distant memory, replaced by restless nights spent staring at the ceiling, replaying Day's last look, searching for clues in his silent farewell.

She found herself drawn to the bustling, chaotic energy of the Roti Shop, a familiar haven in this sea of uncertainty. The rhythmic chomping of the mortar and pestle the cheerful banter of Papa Ram and Mama Sita, the comforting aroma of spices – these were anchors in the storm, reminders of a life shared, a life she was desperately clinging to. But even here, the shadow of Day's absence loomed large, a constant reminder of the precariousness of their situation.

Maddaar appeared during one of Adelyn's most despondent moments, a ghostly figure materializing from the shadows of the alleyway. He didn't offer words of comfort, nor did he make promises. His silent presence, however, was a calming force, a tacit acknowledgement of her pain. He simply sat beside her, sharing her silence, his eyes reflecting the same turbulent emotions churning within her. He understood the language of loss, the unspoken grief that bound them together. The official charges were laid – breaking and entering, possession of stolen goods, the usual litany of accusations that had become synonymous with Day's life.

Visiting Day in prison, Adelyn found herself plunged into a bleak abyss. The jail, a chilling monument to human suffering, mirrored the crushing weight of Day's incarceration. A suffocating atmosphere of despair hung heavy, an oppressive blanket stifling all hope. Even the meager rays of sunlight felt cruelly ironic. Though Day kept a façade of defiance, her spirit was visibly fracturing under the unrelenting pressure. Adelyn's presence a fleeting disruption in the stagnant silence evoked a harrowing, unspoken communion of anguish.

Her usual vibrancy was gone, replaced by the hesitant movements of a wounded creature. Their embrace, a desperate plea for solace, spoke volumes. Adelyn traced the lines etched by suffering onto Day's face, her carefully chosen words of comfort masking a rising tide of unspoken fear. Day's brittle reassurance was a fragile shield against the crushing reality. The silence between them, heavy with unspoken grief, was more agonizing than any words. As their time dwindled, the impending separation felt like a physical blow. Their final touch, a desperate clinging to a tenuous connection, underscored the profound sorrow of their shared predicament.

The final, wrenching goodbye was a silent scream, a desperate prayer hanging in the air, thick with the bitter scent of loss and the chilling promise of uncertainty. The heavy clang of the steel door, echoing again, was the final, crushing blow, leaving both broken, bleeding, and clinging to the frayed edges of hope. His eyes held a spark of determination, a flicker of hope amidst the bleakness. But Adelyn saw the cracks in his armor, the strain etched into the lines of his face.

Aunt Hilda's jarring words, "He's gone," scraped raw a wound already bleeding grief. Hilda's cloying perfume felt like a cruel slap; her touch equally inadequate. "No," Adelyn choked, clutching a trembling teacup – a pale reflection of her shattered life. "He can change," she whispered, clinging to a fading echo. Hilda sighed, her pity masking a weary understanding of Adelyn's defiant, doomed love, a love that burned even brighter in the ashes of loss. The unspoken words hung heavy, a testament to a beauty tragically destroyed. a love born amidst stolen glances and whispered promises in the dimly lit alleys of Suva, a love that burned bright despite the constant threat of separation, the ever-present fear of his next arrest. He was her storm, her tempest, a whirlwind of passion and danger that both terrified and captivated her. Yet, a part of her, a pragmatic, cautious part, screamed for escape, for a life free from the anxiety, the sleepless nights spent worrying about his whereabouts, and the constant fear of a phone call delivering devastating news.

28

The visits became her lifeline, a brief respite from the gnawing anxiety that threatened to overwhelm her. She brought him roti and prawn curry, his favorite, a small act of defiance against the harsh reality of his situation, a testament to their enduring love. The simple act of sharing a meal, across the cold, impersonal barrier of the prison visiting room, was a powerful act of affirmation, a reaffirmation of their bond.

Adelyn's legal battle was a torturous crawl through bureaucratic indifference. The stale courtroom air, thick with resentment, mirrored her dwindling hope. Then, the clerk, Jagdish Lal– a man of granite coldness – slammed her denied petition onto his desk. His dismissive words, dripping with disdain, confirmed her fears. The brittle paper felt like her shattered hopes, the crushing weight of the legal system leaving her hollow. But a controlled rage simmered beneath her mask; this fight wasn't over. Adelyn, armed with her own unwavering determination, navigated the complexities of the Fijian legal system, a system she knew little about but was quickly learning to navigate. She spent countless hours poring over legal documents, seeking advice from sympathetic lawyers and family members, employing every ounce of her determination to secure Day's release.

During one of their visits, Day confessed a truth he'd kept hidden, a secret that cast a new layer of complexity onto their relationship. He revealed the extent of his criminal activities and the depth of his involvement in the underworld of Suva. He admitted to actions that went beyond petty theft, actions that involved far greater risks and consequences. His confession, though painful, was also a testament to his honesty and his commitment to transparency, even in the face of

29

despair. It was a vulnerability that brought them closer, solidifying the already unbreakable bond between them. The weight of his actions, the consequences of his choices, pressed heavily on Adelyn. She questioned their future, the viability of a life together amidst the ever-present shadow of his criminal past. Yet, amidst the uncertainty, a fierce resolve took root within her. Her love for Day, a tenacious and unwavering force, pushed her forward. She refused to abandon him, to let his past define their present or future.

Day's trial was a brutal clash between his exceptional talent and the relentless force of the law. The courtroom throbbed with tension; fear and anticipation hung heavy. Prosecutor Goundar, a hawk-like figure, branded Day a predator, exploiting the vulnerable. A murmur of outrage followed. Defense attorney Tuwai countered, arguing Day was a victim of systemic failure, not a monster. Then Adelyn testified—her words a bombshell. Her usually cheerful voice, now strained with love and terror, described Day's support despite its questionable origins. Goundar's icy cross-examination highlighted Adelyn's dependence on Day's ill-gotten gains. Adelyn's unwavering belief in his potential for change was heart-wrenching. The judge's gavel punctuated the charged silence. Day and Adelyn exchanged a desperate, silent plea across the room. The verdict's impending weight—would love triumph over justice, or would hope to be extinguished? The silence was suffocating. Her unwavering support, her belief in his potential for redemption, became a powerful counterpoint to the prosecution's narrative.

The verdict came down like a guillotine, a harsh sentence that left Adelyn reeling. Day's incarceration, far from being a mere setback, felt like a death sentence to their fragile dreams of a life together. The reality of his prolonged absence loomed large, casting a long shadow over their future. Yet, even in this darkest hour, a stubborn ember of hope remained. Adelyn, armed with her love and her unwavering faith in Day prepared to fight for their future, a future where love might conquer even the most formidable of adversaries.

The fight was far from over; it was just beginning. The Roti Shop, the bustling streets of Suva, and the cold, unforgiving walls of the prison – all were battlegrounds in the ongoing war for their love, a battle that would evaluate the limits of their resilience and the depth of their commitment.

Prison Life and Adelyn's Steadfastness

Oppressive humidity hung heavy, a suffocating blend of sweat, fetid corruption, and profound despair. Day Marshall squeezed into a cell barely larger than a coffin and felt the weight of it pressing down on him, a physical manifestation of his guilt and regret. The corrugated iron walls, slick with condensation, reflected the flickering fluorescent lights above, casting grotesque shadows that danced with the rhythm of his racing heart. This wasn't the glamorous life he'd envisioned; the life he'd promised Adelyn. This was the cold, hard reality of his choices.

Day's days were a monotonous grind: porridge, marching, guards' shouts, and fleeting sleep. But the routine was a cage, its bars digging deeper daily. A cruel inner voice mirrored the guards' cruelty, amplifying his fears and whispering of weakness, futility, and the folly of hope. Small acts of defiance, like sharing a mango, offered brief resistance against the encroaching darkness but couldn't quell his inner turmoil. Exploiting his despair, the guards offered a deal: inform, gain comfort, and betray his community. The choice ravaged his conscience, but hunger and his internal torment wore him down. He succumbed, revealing an escape plan. The immediate relief – better food, a warmer blanket – was a cruel joke. Overwhelming guilt replaced it; he'd betrayed his friends and, worse, himself. The victory tasted like ash, a testament to his inner enemy's power and his perceived weakness. The monotonous cycle resumed, now poisoned by self-loathing.

He missed the vibrant chaos of the Roti Shop, the aroma of frying fish and *taro*, and the comforting warmth of Adelyn's presence. He missed the feel of her hand in his, the sound of her laughter, the way her eyes held a depth that mirrored the ocean surrounding Suva. He found solace in the small things – the fleeting glimpse of the sky through a barred window, the shared smile with a fellow inmate, the quiet hum of the unseen world outside. But these were mere crumbs of comfort, insufficient to fill the gaping void left by Adelyn's absence. He thought of her constantly – her unwavering dedication, her gentle touch, her fierce spirit that seemed to burn even brighter in the face of his failings.

Adelyn's letters were his lifeline, fragile fragments of hope piercing his prison's suffocating grey. Each page, vibrant with fierce love and longing, shattered the concrete walls. Her precise words painted vivid scenes: the raw struggle for life at CWM Hospital, the Suva market's riotous colours, the sea's tantalizing scent all sensory assaults against his confinement. He lived vicariously through her descriptions, feeling the sun and tasting the salt spray. Adelyn, his valiant sweetheart, fought his battles externally, her strength. masking a vulnerability that tore at his soul. Excerpt from a letter: "My love, the hibiscus is blooming, a furious red against the relentless blue. Today, I held a hand so small it could fit within my palm, a tiny fighter winning their own silent war. It reminded me of your strength, the way you fight your own battles, even here in this darkness. I felt the faintest hint of your spirit in that tiny hand, keeping me going, keeping me breathing for you... for *us*. Don't you dare give up, my love, not while I still have breath in my body to fight for you. The city awaits our return, and my heart aches, pounding a steady rhythm against the cage that separates us. I dream of you every night... I can almost taste your lips, the familiar feel of your hand."

But woven through her descriptions were threads of worry, of a love assessed to its limits. She questioned his actions, not with accusation, but with a profound sadness that pierced him to the core. Each letter was a moving reminder of the chasm that separated them, a gulf carved by his recklessness. He yearned to assure her, to prove to her that he was worthy of her steadfast love, but words felt inadequate, pale imitations of the remorse that churned within him.

One particularly humid afternoon, as he sat listlessly on his cot, a sliver of hope flickered in his heart. A new inmate, a wiry man, Aisea, with kind eyes and a quiet demeanor, shared a story about a lawyer named Mr. Naidu who specialized in cases involving less serious offenses. This lawyer had a reputation for helping inmates negotiate reduced sentences. The news ignited a spark of determination. Perhaps, just perhaps, there was a way out, a way back to Adelyn. He studied the letters Adelyn sent, absorbing her stories, her observations, and everything she shared. He wrote back, detailing his regrets, his plans, and his unwavering love.

Prison rules severely limited Adelyn's visits. Yet, their fleeting meetings ignited a fierce love. Across the stark table, their eyes found comfort. She brought The Fiji Times, its ink bled ghostliness, whispered of sun-scorched days. The photograph of the sea, the turquoise water a searing assault on the senses and crushed between its brittle newspaper pages, a hibiscus, it's crimson dust a poignant perfume of decay, a ghost of a scent that clawed at his throat, a phantom kiss from a paradise lost.

These weren't mere souvenirs; they were shards of a life shattered, a love betrayed, each a brutal, beautiful reminder of a past he could taste, smell, and feel, a past that still bled into his present, a relentless, exquisite torture.

The gnawing doubt twisted in her gut: Should she risk another visit, knowing the pain of separation would only deepen? But the memory of their shared gaze, a beacon in the prison's bleakness, pushed her forward. She was a constant presence, even in her absence. His thoughts constantly circled around her, her unwavering faith in him, even amidst his repeated betrayals. The strength of her love became a fuel for his own self-improvement, a reason to battle the despair of incarceration. Driven by self-improvement, he pursued computer programming classes, diligently striving for mastery. He cultivated reconciliation with his fellow prisoners, fostering a sense of camaraderie. Even the intricate art of weaving, tried with awkward, fumbling hands under the coaching of a seasoned inmate, became a testament to his unwavering commitment to personal growth.

Outside the prison walls, Adelyn's life was a constant battle. Her colleagues at CWM Hospital, though supportive, couldn't fully comprehend the emotional turmoil she endured. The weight of her loyalty to Day, the burden of his choices, gnawed at her. She found herself defending him, even when, deep down, she was struggling to reconcile her love with her frustration. It was a constant tug-of-war, a battle between heart and head that left her perpetually exhausted.

Nights were the hardest. Sleep offered little respite; instead, she was plagued by dreams, vivid and unsettling, of Day trapped behind bars, of his despair, of her own helplessness. The constant worry etched lines onto her face, a subtle testament to the toll his life was taking on her. Yet, even in her darkest moments, she refused to give up hope. She clung fiercely to the belief that Day would change, that their love was strong enough to withstand the storm.

She remembered their first meeting, in the warm glow of the Roti Shop, the electric spark that ignited between them amidst the clatter of plates and the murmur of conversations. It had felt like a fairytale, a love story unfolding in a vibrant, chaotic backdrop. Now, the fairytale felt tainted, the magic replaced by the harsh reality of his life of crime and her unwavering commitment.

The days and weeks stretched into months, each one. punctuated by a carefully worded letter, a fleeting visit, and the unspoken hope for a brighter tomorrow. Adelyn's Steadfast support, her unwavering faith, and her refusal to let go provided Day with the strength to confront his past, to grapple with his demons, and to look forward to a future that could finally be shared with the woman he loved more than life itself. Their connection transcended the physical. Distance, a testament to the strength of their love, a love that even the cold, harsh reality of a Suva Central prison could not extinguish.

Suva's Undercurrents

Suva's oppressive humidity draped itself over everything, a suffocating weight upon the flesh. The scent of salt and diesel, a familiar perfume of the waterfront, mingled with the sweeter, more insidious aroma of rot and decay from the overflowing bins behind the Roti Shop. From his perch above the bustling eatery, Day could almost taste the city's undercurrents, the simmering tensions and deals that pulsed beneath the veneer of everyday life.

His release had been swift, almost anticlimactic. Following a lengthy imprisonment, his liberation arrived with unexpected speed, a sudden anticlimax. The magistrate, a stout judge, Ismail, glistening with perspiration despite the chilled air condition, perfunctorily signed his documents, a world-weary groan emanating from his lips. Freedom, however, felt less like a triumphant escape and more like a reprieve, a temporary stay of execution. The shadows of his past, the ghosts of his former associates, still lurked in the alleyways and shadowed corners of Suva.

Day had known Maddaar for years – a shadowy figure haunting Suva's Streets. His identity, hidden behind a hat and glasses, was a mystery. Unlike Day's petty thievery, Maddaar controlled Suva's criminal underworld, its unseen director. He dealt not in stolen goods but in influence, manipulating fortunes and reputations. His reach extended through every level, brokering deals and silently orchestrating events to support his power.

Whispers spoke of his ties to corrupt officials and wealthy elites, his invisible hand guiding Suva's descent into organized crime. Maddaar was Suva's hidden heart of darkness.

Day found Maddaar in his usual haunt, a dimly lit backroom of a *Trap's Bar* nestled in a labyrinthine alley off Victoria Parade. The air was thick with the smell of cheap rum and desperation. Maddaar sat at a corner table, a half-empty basin of kava beside him, his fingers tracing intricate patterns on the worn tabletop. He didn't look up as Day approached.

"You're out," Maddaar stated, his voice a low rumble as if the words were being drawn from the depths of the earth itself. He didn't offer a greeting, no pleasantries, just a blunt observation. "*Bula,* ya, for now," Day greeted taking a seat opposite him. He felt the weight of Maddaar's gaze, a silent pressure that demanded attention. "They're looking for you, Day," Maddaar continued, his voice barely audible above the raucous laughter and clinking glasses from the main bar. "The usual suspects. And some new ones. They're more…thorough." A chill snaked down Day's spine. "Thorough, how?"

Maddaar smirked, a fleeting glimpse of something sharp and calculating behind his dark glasses. "They're not interested in the small stuff anymore. They want the big fish. And you, my friend, are swimming in the deepest part of the ocean."

The "usual suspects" were the other safecrackers, the low-level thieves who ran within Suva's network. They were expendable and easily replaced, but they were also the ones who kept the city's underbelly running smoothly. The new ones, however, were the ones Day feared. They were the ones who moved in the shadows, the ones with the connections that extended beyond the borders of Fiji. Maddaar's words painted a grim picture. Day's release wasn't an ending; it was a new beginning, a perilous dance with fate. He needed to disappear, to vanish from the city's radar before they found him. But where could he go? Suva was his home, and despite its dangers, it was also the only place he knew.

He thought of Adelyn, the unwavering anchor in his turbulent life. Her unshakeable belief in his ability to change, to break free from his criminal past, had been the driving force behind his decision to turn himself in. But now, her faith was tested once more. He couldn't risk dragging her into this darkness. He had to protect her, even if it meant sacrificing his own safety.

He spent the next few days moving like a phantom through the city's labyrinthine streets, his movements guided by instinct and years of experience in avoiding detection. He met with contacts in dimly lit bars and back alleys, paying off debts and securing safe houses. He relied on a network of informants; each contact a small piece of a larger puzzle that helped him navigate the dangerous waters of Suva's underworld. Clammily sweating, he inhaled the cloying jasmine and a metallic tang – the scent mirroring the icy dread gripping him. He knew the "new ones" weren't amateurs; a Singaporean syndicate, efficient and ruthless, masked its ambition behind legitimate businesses: the National Bank of Fiji. Their meticulously planned heist, a symphony of calculated risk, involved compromised insiders, cleverly substituted vault components, and laundered donations. The supposedly impenetrable bank vault, a legend of titanium and multi-layered security, was their target. Mr. Lee, the syndicate's leader, had a chilling reputation for cracking the uncrackable. This wasn't theft; it was a shadow war, a silent battle for control where lives were expendable. A pawn in this deadly game, Day felt the syndicate's crushing weight, the humid air a cruel mockery of paradise lost. Yet, Day knew the vault's flaws – a tempting siren song promising wealth and freedom.

This new threat was unlike anything Day had faced before. They were ruthless, efficient, and incredibly well-connected. They worked outside of the traditional Fijian criminal. networks, using sophisticated technology and cold, Calculated precision to achieve their goals. Their methods were brutal, and their reach extended far beyond the confines of Suva.

As Day delved deeper into the underbelly of Suva, he encountered a cast of characters as colorful and complex as the city itself: Crawford, the aging bar owner with a penchant for gossip and a surprising network of informants; Villi, the streetwise young pickpocket with a surprising talent for escaping the police; Raju, the disgruntled security guard with inside information on the bank's security system; and the enigmatic Maddaar, ever present, ever watchful, pulling the strings from the shadows.

Suva clawed at him, a beast of beauty and brutality. The city itself was a character, a venomous serpent coiled around a heart of gold. Its vibrant markets, a riot of color and scent, assaulted his senses: the sticky sweetness of mangoes melting on his tongue, the acrid bite of chili powder stinging his nostrils, the suffocating perfume of frangipani flowers battling with the stench of rotting fish from the harbor. The rhythmic pulse of the nightclub's drums, a seductive bass thrumming through the cracked pavement, vibrated in his chest, a stark counterpoint to the chilling silence that hung heavy in the shadowed alleyways.

Each sarong, a kaleidoscope of color, hid a story – tales of fierce independence and desperate survival whispered in the rustle of pure cotton. The laughter of children playing in the dust mingled with the guttural growl of a fight breaking out just beyond the flickering neon signs. His skin prickled; the heat hung thick and humid, a palpable tension clinging to the air like the clinging perfume of jasmine. Even the sea, a Sapphire expanse under the brutal sun seemed to mirror the city's duality, its calm surface hiding the treacherous currents below. This wasn't just a city; it was a crucible, forging souls in its fiery heart. He felt the city's pulse – a frantic heartbeat of life and death, joy and sorrow – throbbing against his own.

The beauty was a cruel deception, a lure into a darkness so profound, so utterly consuming, that it threatened to swallow him whole. The violence, sharp and sudden like a cane knife, was ever-present, a silent predator lurking just beyond the reach of the flickering streetlights. And in that suffocating duality, in that exquisite and terrifying dance between light and shadow, he found himself changed, marked forever by the raw, untamed soul of Suva.

Day's investigation took him to the seedy corners of Suva, where the city's underbelly thrived: the smoky backrooms of gambling dens, the dimly lit bars frequented by criminals and informants, the shadowy alleys where deals were struck, and betrayals were common. He met with informers, gathered intelligence pieced together the puzzle of the Singaporean syndicate's operation. The more he learned, the more dangerous his situation became.

The city's underbelly was a tapestry woven from threads of greed, ambition, and desperation. Each character, each interaction, added another layer to the complexity of Suva's hidden world, highlighting the moral ambiguities and the fine line between right and wrong that defined Day's existence. His life, like the city itself, was a juxtaposition of beauty and brutality, of love and betrayal, of hope and despair.

He knew the inherent danger a mortal threat to both him and Adelyn in confronting this powerful syndicate. But to do nothing guaranteed a far more devastating result. He was determined to forge a counterstrategy, a subtle and intricate plot to expose their wicked machinations, to publicly unveil their corruption, and finally to shatter their reign of terror. But doing so would require a level of cunning and daring that even he was unsure he had. His time in prison had given him a renewed perspective, but it hadn't erased his past, nor had it lessened the dangers that awaited him. The gamble was huge, the stakes even higher. Suva's undercurrents pulsed with anticipation, a deadly rhythm that dictated his next move. The city held its breath.

Adelyn's Growing Frustration

The sterile scent of antiseptic couldn't mask the bitter taste in Adelyn's mouth. Another late night at CWM Hospital, another frantic call from the police, another agonizing wait before the familiar dread settled – Day was in trouble again! This time, it was a jewelry store heist gone wrong, a clumsy attempt, she'd heard whispered amongst the officers, a blatant disregard for caution that bordered on recklessness.

Her colleagues, ever so discreetly, offered hushed condolences and sympathetic glances. They knew her life was a rollercoaster of stolen moments and shattering disappointments, a love story punctuated by the clang of prison bars.

The rhythmic beeping of heart monitors provided a morbid counterpoint to the frantic turmoil in her chest. Each beep was a reminder of Day's precarious existence, and a life balanced precariously on the edge of a knife, a life she loved fiercely, yet a life that threatened to consume her whole.

She scrubbed at a stubborn stain on a blood-soaked sheet, the repetitive motion a desperate attempt to cleanse the grime not just from the linen but from her own soul. The stain mirrored the persistent blot on their relationship, a dark mark she couldn't seem to erase.

She pictured him, his usually mischievous eyes clouded with fear, his hands – those nimble hands that could unlock any door, any heart – bound tightly behind his back. The thought twisted a fresh knot in her stomach. He'd promised her, again and again, that this time would be different. Each promise, delivered with a desperate sincerity that melted her heart, was followed by a crushing betrayal. She was tired. Exhausted, drained of the energy needed to forgive, to hope, to even simply endure. The weight of her frustration was immense, a physical burden that pressed down on her chest, making it hard to breathe. The rhythmic pulse of the city, the distant sounds of the Suva night, seemed to mock her quiet despair. They whispered tales of Day's exploits, of his daring escapes and audacious heists, but they stayed silent on the heartbreak he left in his wake. Each successful job, each narrow escape, seemed to push her further away, widening the chasm. Between them. The memory hit her like a gut punch, a wave of scent – ripe mangoes bruised and fermenting, the cloying sweetness battling the sharp tang of the sea air – washing over her. She saw them again, young and reckless, their stolen kisses under the heavy-laden mango boughs, a taste of forbidden fruit both sweet and bitter on her tongue. The laughter, once a bright, carefree melody echoing through the cacophony of Suva's markets – the guttural cries of vendors, the rhythmic thud of coconuts cracking, the brassy clang of a distant temple bell – now felt like a cruel mockery.

An elusive, shimmering future relentlessly haunted Adelyn, its phantom presence a constant companion. Her family remained largely oblivious to the turmoil consuming her. Her grandmother, the matriarch, had explicitly warned Adelyn to avoid Day. The prestigious *Nath family*, cornerstones of Fijian Indian society, shouldered the weighty legacy of their illustrious past – a heritage both magnificent and suffocating. A single blemish, a concealed indiscretion, menaced their reputation, threatening to taint their unwavering piety and meticulous devotion. Their once-bright prospects hung precariously, poised to disintegrate and rot like overripe mangoes abandoned to the scorching Fijian sun. The midday Sunday service at the Methodist church served as a stark stage upon which the aristocratic Nath family displayed their prominent status, a spectacle of both privilege and vulnerability.

He'd been a storm, beautiful and destructive, leaving behind only the wreckage of her naive belief in a life beyond the shadow of their violent heritage. The weight of that legacy, heavy as a stone tied to her ankle, pulled her back to the murky depths, a constant reminder of the inescapable truth: some shadows are impossible to outrun.

Betrayal and despair, a venomous cocktail, ignited a furious inferno within Adelyn. Crushing hopelessness and a paralyzing terror seized her, suffocating her very essence. She tasted blood and sensed decay, yet a buzzing bumblebee near a dying sunflower sparked a choked chuckle. It's absurd tenacity, a tiny defiance against overwhelming odds offered a fleeting whisper of hope, a reminder that life, however absurd, persists even amidst the wreckage. She loved Day with an intensity that both thrilled and terrified her. His charm was undeniable, a potent mix of roguish humor and vulnerability that drew her in, time and time again. But his love was a dangerous game, one she was increasingly reluctant to play.

The hospital's fluorescent lights cast long shadows across her weary face as she replayed her last conversation with him. A rushed phone call from the police station, a mumbled apology,

45

a whispered promise to change. Words that had lost their meaning, hollow promises repeated like a broken record. She longed for a genuine change, not just another fleeting moment of remorse, another temporary reprieve before the cycle began anew. Her colleagues, noticing her distress, offered words of comfort, but their platitudes felt like empty gestures. They couldn't comprehend the intricate dance of love and fear that consumed her, the agonizing pull between her desire to stand by him and her desperate need to escape the suffocating grip of his lifestyle. They saw a woman hopelessly entangled with a criminal; a cautionary tale played out under their noses. But Adelyn saw something more – a man capable of great love, a man trapped in a self-destructive cycle, a man she desperately wanted to rescue from himself.

The next morning brought a wave of fresh exhaustion, the kind that settled deep in the bones and refused to lift. She trudged through her work, the familiar routines a dull ache rather than a comfort. The faces of her patients, their stories of pain and suffering, became a reflection of her own internal battle. Each bandage she carefully applied, each wound she tended, felt like a metaphor for the countless emotional wounds she was trying to heal. During a lull in the busy ward, she found herself staring out the window. The city of Suva spread before her, a tapestry of vibrant colors and hidden shadows. The thought of Day, confined within the cold walls of a prison cell, struck her with renewed force. His incarceration wasn't just a temporary setback; it was a symbol of their broken relationship, a constant reminder of the chasm that separated them.

Overwhelming frustration threatened to consume her. Day's perilous life, marked by violence and shadows, had hardened him, etching weariness onto his face. Her anger wasn't solely directed at him but at the cruel fate binding them. A deeper resentment gnawed—she'd vowed to avoid this life, yet here she was, complicit in his dangerous game. Was this love or misguided loyalty? Her carefully constructed morality battled with her affections. She faced a brutal choice: support Day, accept the moral compromises, or abandon him to a worse fate. Leaving him felt like a soul-crushing betrayal, yet staying meant a slow descent into the darkness she'd always shunned. Guilt clawed at her; even her small acts fueled the fire. The potential for future compromises filled her with dread. She felt she'd failed to protect herself and her ideals. Then, Day's gentle touch, a flicker of his old playful self in his weary eyes, offered a tiny spark of hope amidst the turmoil. This small gesture, a brief respite in her internal war, momentarily eased her despair, giving her strength to navigate the treacherous currents of her choice.

The city, vibrant and chaotic, seemed to reflect her inner turmoil. The sounds of car horns, the chatter of the street vendors and the distant rhythm of Fijian music – all blended into a discordant symphony that mirrored the conflict emotions within her heart. She knew she couldn't simply walk away, not without a fight, not without trying to save the man she loved. But how could she save him when he seemed determined to destroy himself?

Maddaar's Cryptic Advice

Day collapsed onto a stool at the Roti Shop, the oppressive Suva humidity clinging to him, a cloying blend of diesel exhaust and the rich aroma of ghee-soaked roti saturating the air. His usual swagger was absent, replaced by a weariness that etched deeper lines onto his already-weathered face. He hadn't slept properly in days, and the fluorescent lights of the police station were in stark contrast to the comforting darkness of his usual rooftop refuge. He nursed a lukewarm bowl of kava, the slightly bitter taste doing little to soothe the turmoil within him.

Adelyn's face swam before his eyes, her usually bright, compassionate gaze clouded with a hurt that cut him deeper than any prison cell. He'd promised her, again, that this would be the last time. This jewelry heist, this a desperate gamble to pay off a mounting debt would be his final act of defiance. But his words felt hollow even to him, the lie clinging to his tongue like the sticky residue of sweet roti dough. He was a thief, a safecracker, a man whose skills were as much a curse as they were a means of survival.

He glanced towards the back of the shop, where the old man Maddaar usually sat, shrouded in shadows and the aroma of his pungent herbal concoctions. Maddaar, was a fixture in the shop, a silent observer of the human drama that unfolded daily within its walls. He'd never overtly judged Day, but his knowing eyes held a depth that hinted at unspoken wisdom, a wisdom Day felt a desperate need to tap into.

He found Maddaar hunched over a small wooden table, his gnarled fingers meticulously sorting through a collection of dried herbs. The air around him hummed with a strange energy, a palpable sense of ancient knowledge. Day approached cautiously, the squeak of his worn sandals a jarring intrusion into the quiet intensity of the old man's world.

"*Bula,* Maddaar," Day began, his voice barely a whisper. He felt the weight of his failures pressing down on him, the crushing weight of Adelyn's disillusionment.

Maddaar didn't look up, his gaze fixed on the herbs as if they held the answers to all the world's mysteries. The silence stretched, punctuated only by the rhythmic sizzle of oil in a nearby wok. The anticipation was almost unbearable.

At last, Maddaar's voice, a gravelly whisper akin to autumn leaves skittering across parched earth, broke the silence. "The ebb, Day Marshall, is inevitable; it always comes. Yet, the boundless sea endures." This mirrored Day's own recent setbacks: his promising business venture, once a surging wave of prosperity, had receded, leaving him stranded on the shore of disappointment. But the vast ocean of his potential, his resilience, his innate capabilities—that remained, unshaken and vast, waiting for the next tide to rise. His words were riddles, shrouded in the same enigmatic aura that surrounded him.

Day frowned, struggling to decipher the meaning behind the cryptic pronouncements. "What do you mean, Maddaar? The tide? The ocean?"

Maddaar chuckled, a dry, rattling sound. "The tide of your life, boy. It pulls you out to sea, then throws you back on the shore. But the ocean, that is the constant. It is the depth of your being, the strength within." He paused, letting the words hang in the air like fragrant incense. "The ocean can be calm, or it can be a raging storm. It can nourish or destroy. It depends on your navigation."

Day sat rigidly, the cold wood biting into his thighs. Maddaar's words weren't just unsettling; they were a brutal revelation. Maddaar had pierced Day's carefully constructed facade, exposing the festering betrayal at his core – a violation of his oath to his love, Adelyn. This wasn't mere unease; it was a maelstrom of guilt. Maddaar's words were a mirror reflecting Day's complicity in Adelyn's ruin, a downfall enabled by his cowardice and ambition. He'd chosen self-preservation over his or her well-being, a monstrous choice now devouring his conscience. The enemy wasn't Maddaar but Day's own selfish hunger for power, a seductive whisper that blinded him to the ethical wreckage.

He'd cloaked self-interest in the guise of the greater good. Maddaar's condemnation forced a stark choice: bury the guilt and solidify his power or risk everything for a desperate, perhaps futile, atonement. Either path felt like damnation. The crushing weight of his failure, both past and future, threatened to suffocate him. He was trapped, consumed by regret. "But how do I navigate, Maddaar? How do I control the storm?" Day's voice was filled with desperation. He needed clarity, a beacon in the darkness that threatened to consume him.

Maddaar's ancient gaze, moonlight-deep, pierced Day's soul. His stillness, a predator's patience, amplified the intensity of

50

his stare. "Day Marshall, your inner compass, not external guidance, dictates your path. Even tumultuous life's storms eventually calm". He picked up a small, smooth, grey stone, its surface worn smooth by the relentless action of the sea. He held it out to Day. "This stone has weathered countless storms. It holds its shape. It remembers the pounding waves. The current may try to pull you under. It may even knock you off course. But do you understand what it does not do?"

Day shook his head, his heart pounding in his chest like a war drum.

"It does not break," Maddaar whispered, his voice heavy with unspoken wisdom. "Just as you, Day Marshall, will not break if you find your own compass. The path is difficult. But the ocean will not consume you unless you let it. Only you can make the journey."

He turned back to his herbs, leaving Day to wrestle with the weight of his cryptic advice. The words lingered, echoing in the dimly lit Roti Shop, a strange blend of warning and hope. The ocean, the tide, the compass within – these were metaphors that resonated with a primal force, stirring something deep within Day's soul. He looked at the smooth grey stone, its unyielding strength a silent testament to resilience.

Days turned into weeks, the weight of Adelyn's disapproval a constant reminder of his transgressions. He tried to stay clean, to avoid the easy money, the allure of the thrill. He started spending more time at the hospital, watching Adelyn work, her hands gentle and sure as she ministered to the sick and injured. He saw her compassion and dedication, and it fueled his desire to change, to become worthy of her love.

That night, the intoxicating fragrance of *lamb pulao*, wafting from the Roti Shop, enticed him irresistibly back, its savory perfume a siren's call to his ravenous hunger. He watched the people come and go, their lives unfolding like chapters in a book he was only beginning to understand. He saw the resilience in their faces, the way they navigated their own storms, their own ocean currents. He saw the strength in their quiet dignity, their perseverance in the face of adversity.

He thought about Maddaar's words, about the compass within. He realized that Maddaar wasn't offering a simple solution but a path to self-discovery, a journey of self-reflection and change. He wasn't just a thief; he was a man capable of love, loyalty, and self-sacrifice. The strength, the resilience, the navigating – it was all within him, waiting to be unlocked.

His past clung to him, a suffocating weight, as inescapable as the relentless, torrential rain that drowns Suva. Day felt it most acutely now, standing before the dilapidated wooden shack – his childhood home, now a haven for Ratu, a notorious drug dealer. Ratu, a man Day had once considered a brother, a man whose youthful loyalty had been shattered by the same brutal circumstances that had shaped Day's life. The police, desperate for information on Ratu's operation, had offered Day a deal: betray his former friend or face charges for past indiscretions – indiscretions Ratu himself had drawn Day into. His gut churned. The humid air felt thick and suffocating.

Day's moral compass spun wildly. He'd sworn never again to compromise his integrity, to let the violence and desperation of his past dictate his future. Yet, here he was, staring at the shack, the scent of rotting wood and something far worse – fear – clinging to him. But there was a new feeling, too: a flicker of hope, a renewed determination. He was still a work in progress, a man grappling with his demons, but for the first time, he sensed a direction. He had found his compass, not in the stars, but in the depths of his own heart and in the unwavering love of the woman who waited patiently for him to find his way home.

He saw a young boy, no older than seven, trying to steal a roti from an unattended tray. The boy's hunger was palpable, his eyes wide with desperation. Day saw himself in that boy, a reflection of his own past, his own desperation. He walked over to the boy and gently stopped him. He bought the boy a pack of 6 rotis and some mango juice. The boy's gratitude was more than any payment Day had received from his criminal activities. He saw a different kind of wealth, a different kind of fulfillment.

Redemption's quiet carpentry proved a deceptive solace for Day. His nimble fingers, once adept at thievery, now crafted value, yet the goodness felt alien a persistent pang. Teaching underprivileged youth, he found a mirror in Maxie, a bright but troubled boy mirroring Day's past. Helping Maxie build an intricately carved box with a hidden compartment, Day recognized Maxie's deceptive intent. Duty clashed with empathy; betraying Maxie echoed a past betrayal, silencing his conscience. He aided in the creation of this clandestine vessel, a catastrophic betrayal of his new path. The Workshop's tranquil rhythm became a cruel mockery of his deafening guilt; he'd built not just a box but his own moral prison. His transformation remained incomplete, fractured by his past, leaving him questioning his deservedness for a better future.

He understood now that Maddaar's advice wasn't about escaping the ocean but about learning to swim, about learning to navigate the currents, both calm and tempestuous. He understood the strength that lies in enduring the storms, emerging battered but unbroken, like the smooth grey stone. It wasn't just about changing his profession. It was about changing himself, his mindset, his very being.

One day, he found Maddaar sitting by the seawall across from the Sukuna Park, watching the waves crash against the rocks. He joined him, sharing a quiet moment of camaraderie and understanding. They didn't speak much, but there was a shared acknowledgment of the complex currents of life, the relentless pull of the tide, and the enduring strength of the ocean. The sun dipped below the horizon, painting the sky in hues of orange and purple. It was a beautiful sunset, a fitting backdrop for a new beginning. Day knew his journey wasn't over. He would always be haunted by his past, but he was determined to navigate his future with greater wisdom, greater compassion, and a newfound sense of purpose. He had found his compass, and he was finally ready to set sail. The ocean may be vast and unpredictable, but he now had the strength, the resilience, and the determination to face whatever it threw his way. He had found his way, not by escaping the storm, but by learning to dance with it.

A Promise of Change

The kava's bitterness lingered on Day's tongue, a familiar echo of the harsh realities he'd faced. He watched the bustling street from the Roti Shop, the vibrant chaos was a stark contrast to the quiet turmoil within him. The promise he'd made to Adelyn hung heavy in the air; a fragile thing easily shattered by the wind of his past. He'd vowed to change, to leave the life of a safecracker behind, but the weight of his history pressed down on him, a constant reminder of the path he'd walked.

He knew Adelyn wouldn't easily forgive him. Her love for him was a powerful current, but it was being eroded by the relentless tide of his betrayals. He'd seen the flicker of doubt in her eyes, the subtle shift in her demeanor, the careful distance she was beginning to place between them. He understood. Trust, once broken, was a delicate thing to repair, often requiring more than words to mend.

Day pushed himself away from the counter, the worn wood groaning under his weight. He walked towards the back of the shop, climbing the narrow wooden staircase leading to his tiny apartment. The air here was thick with the smell of damp wood and stale roti, a familiar, comforting scent that had become synonymous with his life. He sat on his worn mattress, the thin fabric offering little comfort. He needed a plan, a tangible way to prove to Adelyn that his words were backed by genuine intention. It wasn't enough to simply say he'd changed; he had to show her. He considered his options. He couldn't simply abandon his skills; his talent for picking locks was ingrained in him, and it was as familiar as the lines on his palm. But he could redirect it. He could use his ability for good, not for gain. The idea sparked a flicker of hope in his chest, a small flame in the vast darkness of his self-doubt.

Melanesian legends, recounted by the enigmatic Maddaar, haunted Day. Tales of Polynesian *sorcery,* imbuing timber with preternatural might, clashed violently with his scientific worldview. Maddaar's whispers of forbidden power echoed in Day's mind, a stark contrast to his rationalism. The solution offered a substance defying modern comprehension yet demanding a human sacrifice was an abhorrent act, a profound violation of Day's ethical principles. Though the ritual yielded a material of incredible, almost miraculous strength, its creation was irrevocably stained by this dreadful act. Maddaar's knowledge, a boundless reservoir of ancient wisdom, offered a glimmer of hope. Day contemplated this vast, forgotten lore, searching for a path to redeem his transgression, to channel his newfound abilities towards constructive ends.

Day embarked on a perilous journey the following dawn, his destination: Maddaar's isolated dwelling, hidden amidst the emerald heart of a remote isle, a mile from the mainland's edge. A tangled, almost impenetrable trail, choked with rampant vegetation, led him through an atmosphere heavy with the perfume of fertile soil and vibrant blossoms, each step a testament to his resolve. He found Maddaar tending to his small garden, his weathered hands working the soil with a gentle grace. Maddaar looked up, his eyes, like ancient pools reflecting the secrets of the forest, met Day's gaze.

"*Bula*, you seek something, Day," Maddaar said, his voice raspy but calm. He had a way of knowing things, of seeing into people's souls. Day hesitated, unsure of how to articulate his predicament. He recounted his struggles, his relationship with Adelyn, and his desperation to change. He spoke of his unique talents, the dark path they had led him down, and his yearning for a path of redemption. He finished, his heart heavy with the weight of his confession.

Maddaar listened patiently, a faint smile playing on his lips. When Day had finished, he rose slowly and led him to a small workshop hidden within the hut. The space was filled with the aroma of polished wood and metal, the tools. Meticulously arranged, each with its own story to tell.

"Your skills are a gift, Day," Maddaar said, "a powerful tool that can be used for creation as well as destruction. It is not the tool, but the hand that wields it." Maddaar showed Day a series of intricate locks, each crafted with a unique complexity, requiring a level of precision and skill that went beyond simple safecracking. They were not locks meant to secure valuables but rather to protect delicate, priceless objects - cultural heirlooms, ancient Artifacts. He spoke of using his knowledge to restore ancient Fijian carvings to help preserve the country's rich cultural heritage. He showed techniques for using his skills to create intricate wooden puzzles, requiring not just nimble fingers but also a keen mind for design and problem-solving.

Day's eyes widened with a newfound understanding. His skills, so often associated with darkness and deceit, could be used to create something beautiful, something lasting. He felt a sense of release, a weightlifting off his shoulders. This wasn't about abandoning his past but about transforming it, about using his unique abilities for something constructive. He learned the ancient art of crafting intricate wooden puzzles, each piece a testament to his renewed purpose.

Days turned into weeks, weeks into months. Day immersed himself in his new craft, finding a sense of peace and purpose he'd never known before. He spent hours in Maddaar's workshop, his hands moving with a newfound grace, his mind focused on the intricate details of his creations. He worked with a passion, transforming his skills into something beautiful and meaningful. He began to sell his creations, small, intricate puzzles that captured the essence of Fijian culture, at the local markets. Word spread quickly, and his pieces were soon sought after by collectors, tourists and enthusiasts alike.

He also helped restore damaged artifacts for the local museum, using his unique skills to repair intricate carvings and locks. His contribution was not merely in his technical skill but also in the pride he took in preserving a part of Fijian heritage. The sense of accomplishment, the knowledge that he was contributing to something positive, filled him with a newfound sense of self-worth.

CWM Hospital's harsh fluorescent hum clashed with the metallic scent of blood clinging to Adelyn's scrubs. Each day was a brutal assault on her senses—death rattles, incessant beeping, antiseptic battling the stench of fear. A ghost in white, she offered surprisingly gentle comfort; her. Reassurances hollow even to herself. "Angel of mercy," they called her, unaware of the leaden weight of her hidden. Despair. Then came Ms. Kiti. The old woman's frail hand, the sorrow in her eyes, shattered Adelyn's composure. A tidal wave of empathy, raw and agonizing, nearly Overwhelmed her. She felt a chilling kinship with Ms. Kiti's suffering recognizes humanity's ability for both profound joy and crushing despair. A sob caught in her throat as she smoothed the old woman's hair; the city's vibrant pulse mocked the icy emptiness within her. Her compassion felt borrowed, drawn from a well she feared. It might be forever depleted. The weight of their unresolved issues lingered, a constant hum beneath the surface of her daily routine. She saw glimpses of Day around town, working at the market, his hands moving with a practiced ease and quiet confidence that was strikingly different from his former swagger.

One day, she saw him in the museum, carefully working on an ancient Fijian canoe, his hands moving with precision and respect. The sight moved her deeply. She saw not the troubled criminal, but a man dedicated to his craft, committed to a positive change. As he finished his restoration work that day, he looked up and caught sight of Adelyn standing near the entrance. Their eyes met, and a myriad of unspoken words passed between them. There was a sense of understanding, a recognition of the immense journey they had both undertaken. The weight of the past hadn't vanished, but it had begun to lighten. It wasn't a sudden, explosive reunion, but the quiet understanding of two souls who had navigated a treacherous storm, scarred but still afloat. It was a beginning, a promise of a future built on trust, resilience, and a shared commitment to a different path. The promise of change wasn't just Day's, and it was theirs.

A Crisis at CWM Hospital

Suva's heavy, humid embrace was thick with the heady fragrance of frangipani, a sensual counterpoint to the city's relentless, vibrant energy. Inside the CWM Hospital, however, the atmosphere was far from tranquil. Chaos reigned. A power surge, followed by a deafening crackle, plunged the entire surgical wing into darkness. The backup generators sputtered, then died, leaving the operating theaters shrouded in an oppressive blackness punctuated only by the frantic glow of emergency flashlights.

Adelyn, her usually calm demeanor replaced with a stark terror, fought her way through the mayhem. The air crackled with static, the rhythmic beeping of heart monitors now erratic and strained. Doctor Mehta and the other Head nurse, Sadhna, shouted instructions over the commotion, their voices strained and desperate. A critical surgery was underway a young boy named, Vaughan, was fighting for his life, his heart barely registering on the dying monitors. The backup power the system, their last hope, was gone. The situation was dire.

Adelyn's heart hammered against her ribs. She remembered the stories Day had told her – tales of his uncanny ability to pick locks, to bypass security systems, tales whispered in hushed tones in the dimly lit Roti Shop above. Tales she had angrily rejected, tales that had fueled countless arguments. Yet here she was, in the heart of a crisis, facing the grim reality that only Day owned the skills to restore the hospital's vital systems.

The image of Day's calloused hands, nimble and quick, flashed through her mind. The same hands that had so deftly picked locks now held the key, quite literally, to this little Vaughan's life. Vaughan, whose tiny hand she'd held just hours before, now lay suspended between life and death, a victim of a power failure and Adelyn's own pride.

The shame stung, bitter, and sharp. She'd judged him, condemned him for his past and allowed her own stubbornness to blind her to the unique talents he possessed. Now, the price of her judgment was being measured in the frantic breaths of a dying child. Her phone, miraculously still functioning on its own battery, felt heavy in her hand as she punched in Day's number, her voice trembling as she spoke.

"Day," she pleaded, her voice barely a whisper above the hospital's cacophony, "it's Adelyn. Please... please, you have to help."

The silence on the other end stretched, an agonizing eternity filled only with the rhythmic thump of her own racing heart.

Little Vaughan's faint heartbeat was barely a whisper in her ear. Adelyn felt tears sting her eyes, blurring the already frantic scene before her. Was this the end? Would her own pride, her own unwillingness to compromise, cost this innocent child his life?

A pause, thick with silence, followed. Then Day's voice, low and measured, cutting through the desperation. "Adelyn, what's wrong? Tell me."

She poured out her fear, the helplessness, the urgency of the

61

situation. She described the failing life support, the dimming lights, the desperate fight to keep little Vaughan alive. She heard the shift in his voice, the hardening of his tone. The familiar guilt that she always felt when he was near, but now it was different, a cold fear replacing the familiar anxiety.

Day's voice, a lifeline tossed onto a raging sea, crackled through the phone, "Stay calm, Adelyn. I'll be there".

The clipped assurance, usually grating on her nerves like chalk on a blackboard, was now a godsend, a raw, urgent promise vibrating in the air. The final click, a metallic *snap* echoing the violent tremor in her own chest, normally a symbol of his infuriating detachment, felt like the hammer blow sealing a desperate pact.

He wasn't far. Just across the churning black water, the skeletal silhouette on Maddaar's island, a jagged tooth against the bruised, twilight sky. From the shadowed cove where he stood, CWM Hospital's sickly yellow glow was visible – a beacon both promising and terrifying.

The rasp of the boat's engine, a guttural beast tearing through the waves, was a symphony of impending arrival. Day, his usual polished composure shattered, a frantic glint in his eyes that mirrored the storm's fury, was already aboard Temo's battered motorboat cutting a frantic path towards her. The reek of gasoline, sweat, and the ocean's brine filled the air – a visceral reminder of his breakneck haste. Temo, a man whose loyalty was as thick and unshakeable as the sea's grip on the island, roared a wordless encouragement over the engine's thunder, his weathered face a grim mask of shared urgency. Every second felt like an eternity, each slap of the waves against the hull a hammer blow to her already fractured heart. This was Day, the infuriatingly enigmatic Day, tearing through the night, his usual controlled façade ripped to shreds by a force more powerful than himself – his *love* for her.

The wait felt interminable. Each second stretched into an eternity. She fought to keep little Vaughan's vital signs stable, her hands working almost automatically, guided by years of training but fueled by a desperate hope. She imagined Day, pictured him navigating the labyrinthine corridors of the hospital, the darkness a familiar cloak to him, a place where he was comfortable moving in the shadows.

He reached the hospital, a cold knot of apprehension. tightening his stomach. The air throbbed with tension, the sounds of panic mingling with the hushed whispers of the medical team. He recognized Adelyn, her face pale and drawn, her eyes filled with a desperate hope that mirrored his own internal struggle.

He navigated the corridors with a grim determination, moving with an unnerving quietness. His steps were deliberate, his movements precise – years spent navigating the city's darker corners had honed him into a shadowy efficiency. The smell of antiseptic and the faint metallic tang of blood filled the air, a harsh reminder of the task before him.

He reached the generator room, his eyes scanning the complex system of locks and security panels. The tension was palpable; the fate of the child hung precariously in the balance. His hands, calloused and scarred, moved with a practiced precision, his fingers dancing across the keypad, his mind a whirlwind of algorithms and codes.

The rhythmic ticking of the emergency clock, a relentless counterpoint to his focused work, was a pressure he knew well. This wasn't just a lock; it was a life, a precious life hanging in the balance. The weight of it all settled on him, a tangible burden. He felt the eyes of Adelyn, the medical staff, and even the silent watchers of this hidden room bearing down on him.

He worked in silence, and the only sounds were the hum of the failing system and the distant cries of the hospital staff. His mind raced, a frantic dance of code and logic. Finally, with a satisfying click, the locks yielded, and the generator whirred to life.

Power surged back into the hospital, restoring the lights and the life-sustaining machines. The relief that washed over the room was palpable, a wave of collective sighs and hushed thanks. Adelyn rushed to his side, her eyes wet with tears of relief. She embraced him, her body trembling with a mixture of gratitude and a raw, visceral understanding of the man she loved.

But even in that moment of triumph, Day knew that this victory was fleeting. His past still clung to him like a shadow a constant reminder of the price he'd paid for his skills. The hospital heist had bought him a temporary reprieve, but his own desperate measures to change, to escape his criminal life, were yet to come. The weight of his past loomed large, the sacrifice he would make to secure a future with Adelyn still hanging heavy in the air, unseen yet inevitable.

Day's Reluctant Return

The ferry's impact on the Suva dock, a jarring collision, sent stinging salt spray across Day's face. His meticulously constructed haven, a fragile illusion built on Adelyn's desperate pleas, crumbled. He had sought refuge on that island, a desperate flight from his past and a looming sense of doom. But Adelyn, his insidious lover, had yanked him back into the maelstrom. Returning meant confronting those privies to his clandestine life, those who craved the destruction of his painfully earned tranquility. A premonition of his own demise gnawed at him, yet Adelyn's precarious existence exerted a more potent force. He was ensnared, agonizing over the choice between an elusive freedom and a love that threatened damnation. The ocean's thunderous roar mirrored the tempest within. His vision of paradise—pristine coral, aquamarine waters, serene stillness—dissolved, supplanted by Suva's noxious atmosphere: a reeking blend of diesel fumes, putrefaction, and the bitter tang of treachery.

The oppressive humidity, a suffocating cloak, amplified his remorse. His sanctuary was reduced to embers, his serenity shattered, and a final confrontation loomed.

The Roti Shop, his home above the bustling diner, felt different, emptier. The vibrant chaos that usually pulsed through the place, the clatter of plates, the cheerful banter of the customers, the rhythmic chomping of the mortar and pestle was muted by a faint echo of its former self. Even the aroma of spices, usually so potent, felt thin, lacking its usual heart. The silence was deafening, mirroring the turmoil inside him.

In his customary alcove, Day discovered Maddaar, cradling a kava bowl. A frail silhouette cloaked in gloom, the elder barely registered Day's arrival. His habitual silence, usually profound, now pressed down with a weighty, unspoken empathy. Maddaar, Day understood, had seen the entirety of his life's arc, the flamboyant excesses, the frantic struggles for atonement. No words were necessary; their eyes met; a shared comprehension of Day's precarious journey silently exchanged. "She needed me," Day finally said, his voice rough from disuse, the words catching in his throat. He felt the weight of his confession, the unspoken consequences hanging heavy in the air. He didn't need to explain the details; Maddaar knew the hospital and knew Adelyn.

Maddaar took a slow sip of kava, the liquid gurgling softly in the *bilo* (drinking bowl made from coconut shell). "The heart is a fickle thing, Day," he finally. murmured, his voice raspy but steady. "It leads us to places we never imagined, both glorious and dark." His eyes, ancient and wise, it held a depth that mirrored the vastness of the ocean.

Day nodded, the silence between them stretching, a comfortable understanding settling between them. He didn't expect advice or judgment from Maddaar; he just needed the quiet solace of his presence, the unspoken support that had always been a lifeline in the storm of his life. He knew he couldn't stay away, not from Adelyn, not from the fear that had gripped her, not from the responsibility that gnawed at his conscience. He couldn't outrun the life he'd created, not yet.

The walk to the hospital felt longer than he remembered. The cacophony of Suva's normally soothing marketplace—the vendors' boisterous haggling, the vibrant saris draped on Indian women fiercely negotiating prices, the throbbing Bollywood beats spilling from a shop—now felt like a brutal attack on his senses, a jarring discord he frantically tried to shut out. His mind was consumed by Adelyn, by the fear that shadowed her eyes, the vulnerability he'd witnessed in the hospital.

He found her in the nurses' station, the familiar scent of antiseptic and disinfectant filling the air. She looked tired, her eyes rimmed with dark circles, her usually vibrant energy subdued. But there was a flicker of something else in her gaze – relief, perhaps, mingled with a hesitant hope. "Day," she whispered, her voice barely audible, her eyes wide with a mixture of surprise and cautious joy. He saw the question in her eyes, a silent plea for answers he wasn't entirely sure he had.

He moved closer, the weight of his past threatening to crush him. He saw the exhaustion etched on her face, the lines of worry around her eyes, reflecting the deafening events of the recent power outage. It was a reminder of the precarious balance that dictated their lives, a constant tug-of-war between love and fear, between hope and despair. "I… I came back," he managed, his voice a low rumble. The words felt inadequate, insufficient to convey the turmoil within him, the clashing desires, the guilt, the overwhelming love that brought him back to this place, to her. Adelyn didn't speak for a moment, her

67

eyes searching his as if trying to decipher the truth hidden beneath the surface. He saw a glimmer of understanding, a hint of forgiveness, but also the lingering doubt, the shadow of his past stretching between them. He understood; he'd earned that doubt.

"The generator," she started, her voice trembling slightly. "It was… it was a miracle. We almost lost little Vaughan…" The words hung in the air, laden with unspoken gratitude but also with a sense of lingering apprehension. Day knew what she meant. The unspoken truth hung. Between them, a silent testament to the precariousness of their relationship. His past cast a long shadow over their present, a constant threat to their fragile happiness. He knew he hadn't earned her forgiveness, not yet. But he'd come back, driven by a love that transcended his flaws, his mistakes, his criminal past. He spent the next few hours helping her catch up on her charting, and the quiet hum of activity in the hospital was a soothing counterpoint to the storm raging inside him. He saw the relief on her face as he helped organize supplies, a subtle shift in her demeanor that spoke volumes.

Later, they walked through the hospital gardens, the scent of jasmine and frangipani filling the air. They didn't talk much, but the shared silence was comfortable, a hinted acknowledgement of the unspoken words that lingered between them. The moonlight bathed the scene in a soft, ethereal glow, casting long shadows that danced like specters of their past. The quiet companionship, the simple act of being together, was enough for now. It was a step, a tiny step in a journey that would be long and arduous, but one that was fueled by love, a love strong enough, perhaps, to overcome even his darkest self. The night air was thick with the scent of salt and hibiscus, the gentle sounds of the ocean a constant murmur in the background. As they stood there, bathed in the silver light of the moon, he could feel the weight of his past pressing down on him. It was a heavy burden, but not one he could escape.

He had returned, not just for Adelyn, but for himself. The escape hadn't worked; he needed to face his demons, not run from them. He knew the road ahead would be a long and difficult one. He knew Adelyn deserved better than a life entangled with his criminal past. But he was here, committed to the fight. It was a commitment he would have to prove with every fiber of his being. This was more than a simple return; this was a rebirth, a chance to prove his worth, not just as a lover, but as a man. The future remained uncertain, clouded by the shadows of his past, but he stood firm, determined to build a future that could outshine the darkness.

The journey to redeem himself, to build a life where his love for Adelyn could flourish, would require more than just his presence; it would require a complete transformation. And that transformation, he knew, would be the hardest challenge of his life. But it was a challenge he was willing to face, a battle he was determined to win. For Adelyn. For himself. For a future, he dared to dream of, a future where love, not crime, defined his existence.

The Safecracking Operation

That night, a heavy, humid shroud enveloped Suva, its oppressive weight clinging to Day like a shroud. The air, thick with the heady perfume of jasmine and the harsh sting of vehicular exhaust, bore down on him as he faced the imposing bulk of CWM Hospital. Adelyn's frantic call still echoed in his ears – a whispered plea laced with desperation. He had promised he would help, and he would. This wasn't about the thrill of the heist, the adrenaline rush of outsmarting a system; this was about Adelyn. This was about proving his love wasn't just words, but a commitment etched in action, forged in the crucible of his own desperate gamble.

His heart hammered against his ribs, a frantic drumbeat against the backdrop of the city's hushed murmurs. He had studied the blueprints – pilfered, naturally – memorized the layout, the security systems, the blind spots. He knew the hospital's rhythms, the predictable ebb and flow of staff and patients, the silent patrols of the security guards. His years of illicit practice had honed his instincts, transforming him into a ghost, a shadow moving silently through the darkness.

He moved with the practiced ease of a seasoned professional, his movements fluid and economical. The tools of his trade – a Slim Jim, a set of picks, a miniature fiber optic camera – felt like extensions of his own body. He'd chosen his entry point carefully – a rarely used service entrance. The entrance, tucked away in the shadows, was almost invisible to the casual observer. The lock, a sturdy, modern affair, presented a challenge but not one he couldn't overcome. His fingers, nimble and sure, danced across the tumblers, the subtle clicks and whirs a silent symphony in the night. Each click brought him closer to his goal, and each turn of the pick was a step closer to Adelyn and closer to redemption. The entrance yielded with a soft sigh, a barely audible whisper in the vastness of the hospital. He slipped inside, the cool air of a storeroom, a stark contrast to the humid night air.

The fluorescent lights hummed overhead, casting a sterile, clinical glow on the polished floor. The smell of antiseptic and disinfectant filled his nostrils, a sharp reminder of the life he was trying to escape. He felt a pang of guilt, a bitter taste in his mouth. This wasn't his place, this world of sterile efficiency and healing. Yet, tonight, it was his battleground, his arena. He navigated the labyrinthine corridors with the stealth of a phantom. The floor plan he'd acquired from Raju, the security guard, was accurate, leading him to the administrative wing, the heart of the hospital's security. His target: the main server room, home to the hospital's critical data and – more importantly – the encrypted files holding the information Adelyn needed. It wasn't just a simple lock this time; it was a vault, heavily reinforced and protected by multiple layers of security.

His fiber optic camera was his eyes, feeding him a live feed of the internal mechanisms of the vault door. The image flickered on his tiny screen, illuminating the complex array of locks and sensors. This wasn't some simple residential lock; it required a precise understanding of electronics, an understanding he'd spent years honing. He carefully inserted a thin probe, bypassing the electronic locks with the same practiced ease he'd displayed at the entrance. Each wire he manipulated was a delicate dance, a risky maneuver. A wrong move could trigger an alarm, drawing unwanted attention.

Sweat beaded on his forehead, a testament to the intensity of the operation. His breath hitched in his throat, a silent prayer for success. He focused, his mind shutting out everything except the delicate task at hand. He felt a sense of urgency, a pressure to succeed that was far more intense than any he'd felt in his previous heists. This wasn't just about money; it was about Adelyn, about proving his worth and his capacity for love and change.

Finally, with a soft click, the electronic locks disengaged. The vault door swung open with a groan, revealing rows upon rows of servers humming quietly in the darkness. The air was thick with the smell of electronics and ozone, a strange mix of sterile and technological. He accessed the server, navigating the maze of files and folders with deft fingers. The encrypted files were tucked away in a hidden directory, protected by multiple layers of security software. But nothing could resist Day's skills.

He worked swiftly and methodically, extracting the files he needed and transferring them to a secure external drive. The cold, metallic feel of the drive sent a shiver down his spine, a physical manifestation of the icy dread gripping his heart. He carefully avoided touching anything else, leaving no trace of his presence, a practiced routine that felt more like a macabre dance than a simple task. He knew he was walking a tightrope; one wrong move could bring the entire operation crashing down, and the weight of that knowledge pressed down on him like a physical burden.

The hospital's confidential Native Land records, secured within impenetrable encryption, weighed heavily on him. Adelyn's impassioned pleas echoed in his mind, a stark portrayal of dire need. Yet, her justification felt profoundly inadequate, a chasm separating her urgency from the ethical compass he desperately looked for. Could her goal truly outweigh this perilous transgression? Or was his judgment clouded by the blinding haze of love, his unwavering allegiance to her?

Secretly, she disclosed the origins of the harmful information: a treacherous plot hatched by the Native Land Trust Board, centered on the very ground beneath CWM Hospital. A discovery of immense import had come into her possession— a revelation capable of righting a grievous wrong and exposing those responsible for the deception. His unwavering belief in Adelyn's probity remained absolute; he was certain she'd never knowingly strayed from the righteous path. Or had she?

Every keypress felt like a violation, each copied file a brand upon his conscience. Assisting Adelyn seemed less a noble deed, more a reckless wager, a capitulation to her emotional coercion. He understood, with chilling certainty, that even triumph would leave an inerasable scar. Adelyn's request – to pilfer the hospital vault's encrypted data – stemmed from her knowledge of his profound love, a love she exploited to induce this transgression. She claimed desperation, but Day sensed a deeper deception, a malevolence far exceeding the land dispute ruse. The files themselves paled in significance compared to the agonizing cost he was paying – a price measured not in data, but in the erosion of his integrity. Hmmmm...what integrity?

Once the files were secured, he reversed his steps, retracing his path with the same quiet precision. He bypassed the security systems with practiced ease, his movements almost balletic in their grace and efficiency. He slipped back out into the night, the hospital looming behind him like a silent sentinel. The city lights blurred into streaks of color as he walked. The cool night air felt different now – lighter, almost celebratory. He'd succeeded. He'd done what he had to do. He slipped out of the hospital as dawn painted the sky with strokes of fiery orange and bruised purple, the city slowly awakening to a new day, oblivious to the clandestine operation that had just unfolded within its walls of the CWM hospital. He made his way back to his small apartment above the roti shop, the success of the heist still fresh in his mind. He'd never felt so alive, so acutely aware of the balance between his criminal skills and his unwavering love for Adelyn. This mission wasn't just a crime; it was an act of love, a desperate attempt to bridge the chasm between his past and his desire for a future with her. That night, he proved to himself that he was capable of more than just breaking locks – he could break free from his past. It was a dangerous game, but he'd played it and won, hoping that this win would be the start of something new, something better.

The weight of the hospital heist pressed upon him, heavier than any stolen jewel or plundered treasure. He knew he'd crossed a line, that this act would continue to cast a long shadow over his life. Yet, this act was born of love, not greed. It was a sacrifice he was willing to make, a gamble on a future he desperately craved – a future free from his criminal ways, a future where he could embrace Adelyn without the shadow of his past looming large. He knew there was still a long way to go; this was just one step, a risky and potentially costly step, on the road to redemption. He looked out into the night, the Suva lights reflecting in his eyes, a quiet determination settling in his heart. The game was far from over, but he was ready for whatever the future might bring.

He placed the external hard drive on his small, worn wooden table, the soft click, a stark contrast to the humming servers of the hospital. His hands trembled slightly, a mixture of exhaustion and exhilaration coursing through his veins. He thought of Adelyn, her face etched with worry, her eyes pleading for help. He'd answered that plea, even if it meant delving deeper into the shadows, reaffirming the uneasy balance between his criminal past and his love for Adelyn. He knew that the line between right and wrong blurred in his world, where love and crime intertwined in a dangerous dance. This operation wasn't just about the technical prowess of cracking a secure system; it was about his fierce determination to prove his worth to Adelyn, to demonstrate the depth of his love and his unwavering commitment to building a future together, a future where crime would have no place.

The morning light found him staring at the drive, the weight of his actions settling heavily upon his shoulders. This wasn't just a simple heist, it was a statement, a desperate plea. whispered in the language of his criminal expertise. A statement of his undying love for Adelyn, a silent vow to change his life, to fight for a future together. He knew that his skills, his unique talents, could be a double-edged sword, capable of great harm and great good. It was a responsibility he had to embrace, a burden he had to carry, walking that tightrope between his past and his future. His love for Adelyn pushed him toward redemption, a path fraught with risk and uncertainty but one he was determined to tread, no matter the cost. The heist had bought him time, a chance to prove that he could change. But it was a chance he knew he couldn't afford to squander.

The future remained uncertain, a kaleidoscope of possibilities, but he looked forward with the kind of determination he had never felt before, a determination fuelled by the burning ember of his love for Adelyn. He was ready to face whatever it held, ready to fight for his love, ready to fight for his future. The drive, heavy as a death sentence, the CWM Hospital's Native Land dispute's incriminating secrets −Adelyn's lifeline, his penance.

He hadn't given it to her directly; it was too risky. Instead, he'd cleverly planted a coded message, a fractured sonnet only she'd deciphered three days ago. Adelyn, his brilliant, enthusiastic love, was his reason. She alone saw past his hardened shell to the guilt-ridden man haunted by past failures – a pawn in the land dispute game, now seeking atonement. This defiance, his reckless attempt at justice, aimed to rebuild from their shared trauma. Failure? The drive's cold weight felt crushing.

Police Investigation

A cloying, tropical dampness permeated Suva, the fragrance of plumeria battling a choking haze of vehicular pollution. The weight of countless unresolved mysteries etched itself onto Detective Inspector Ravinesh Singh's countenance as he assessed the grim scene. CWM Hospital, usually a beacon of hope, was now shrouded in a suffocating blanket of despondency.

The shocking discovery of an unauthorized entry into the server room by the night shift technicians revealed a sinister aim: the theft of irreplaceable Native Land Trust documents, meticulously preserved within the hospital's secure data vault. These vital records, chronicling the hospital's history for generations, detailed the land's ownership back to its earliest days.

The irony wasn't lost on Singh; a place dedicated to saving lives had become the victim of a crime. His team, a mix of seasoned officers and eager recruits, buzzed around him, meticulously documenting the scene. Fingerprints were dusted, security footage reviewed, and statements taken from shaken staff members. The break-in itself was remarkably clean, almost surgical in its precision. No forced entry, no signs of a struggle, just a lingering scent of expensive cologne – something distinctly unfamiliar to the usual suspects they dealt with in Suva's underbelly. Singh recognized the signature of a professional, someone with skills far beyond the run-of-the-mill burglar. The meticulousness suggested someone who knew exactly what they were looking for.

The first reports pointed to an inside job, but Singh remained skeptical. The security system, while outdated, hadn't been bypassed. The thief had circumvented it with an elegance that defied simple opportunism. Someone had orchestrated this with alarming ability. His mind drifted back to the recent spate of seemingly unrelated smaller burglaries, all bearing a similar, unnervingly clean execution. Could this be connected? He felt a prickle of unease, a sensation that this was something bigger, more sinister than a simple heist.

Singh and his team pursued a labyrinthine investigation, each discovery deepening the enigma. Subtle, almost ethereal traces—a barely visible abrasion on a seldom-used access point, a dislodged floorboard in a forgotten storeroom— appeared. Individually insignificant, these fragments coalesced into a compelling narrative, implicating a perpetrator having exceptional dexterity and an encyclopedic understanding of the hospital's infrastructure. Though the proof remained indirect, the proximity to the truth resonated powerfully.

A critical development in the case materialized by chance: a cryptic, ominous note, crudely etched onto a bus shelter near Day Marshall's beloved roti establishment. This brief communication, unnervingly precise in its details, revealed insider knowledge of the robbery—information exclusively owned by the culprit.

It was enough to call for a visit to the Roti Shop. Singh, accompanied by his most trusted officer, Sergeant Bale, approached the building, a familiar yet somehow alien environment. The air buzzed with the sounds of frying onions and the chatter of locals, a stark contrast to the sterile environment of the hospital. A clash of aromas assaulted Singh's senses: the savory fragrance of fried fritters and fragrant, masala chai battled a stale miasma of flat beer and despair, a heady, oppressive cocktail he knew all too well.

The Roti Shop's owner, Mama Sita, a woman with kind eyes and a perpetually worried expression, recounted the few instances where she had seen Day in the days preceding the heist. He had seemed more subdued than usual, his usually vibrant spirit dimmed by a heavy cloud of melancholy. There was nothing suspicious, she insisted, but the subtle change in his demeanor was undeniable. This was a man known for his bravado, his swagger. Now, he seemed withdrawn, his movements almost hesitant.

Singh's mind raced. Day Marshall, a man known for his dexterity and knack for opening anything from a simple padlock to a high-security vault. The anonymous tip, the parallels between the hospital heist and Day's past exploits, were too coincidental to ignore. Yet, the very idea of Day being involved in such a meticulously planned crime seemed improbable.

Their attention then turned to Maddaar, the mystifying recluse, whose cryptic words and ambiguous presence hung over the entire narrative. He was a shadowy figure, a whisper in the community, his past shrouded in mystery. Yet, his knowledge of Suva's underbelly and his connection to Day were undeniable. Ravinesh Singh knew he needed to talk to Maddaar but finding him was proving to be as elusive as the truth itself. Maddaar was a ghost, a phantom lurking in the shadows of Suva, appearing and disappearing at will, leaving a trail of riddles and enigmatic pronouncements in his wake.

Sergeant Bale, the younger officer but one with impressive street smarts, suggested looking into Day's past, digging deeper into the records of his earlier incarcerations. He believed that the key to understanding this current crime lay in understanding Day's history, in the shadowy corners of his past that he had carefully concealed. Singh agreed, knowing that the meticulous nature of the hospital break-in suggested a familiarity with the system, a knowledge honed over years of careful planning and calculated risks.

The investigation into Day's past led them to a network of contacts, informants and ex-convicts, each contributing a piece to the puzzle. The picture that appeared was one of a man driven by desperation, a man who had once owned unparalleled skill as a safecracker, an expert in his craft, but one who had also been betrayed, framed for a crime he had not committed. This betrayal had pushed him to the edge, fueling his vengeful actions, transforming him from a skilled artisan into a calculating criminal.

The investigation didn't directly implicate Day in the hospital heist but revealed a pattern – a meticulously planned sequence of crimes that culminated in the hospital break-in.

Each crime had involved gaining access to sensitive information, information that was later used to further another crime. It was a sophisticated operation, a web of interconnected crimes, only detectable through meticulous observation and piecing together disparate clues. The real goal was far more sinister, more deeply ingrained in the corruption that had begun to fester within the city's administrative system. It was a shocking discovery that implicated figures far higher than Day could have ever reached.

Another breakthrough. They discovered a connection between the hospital records and a major land development deal, one shrouded in secrecy and rife with potential corruption. The stolen records held sensitive information that could have been used to extort officials, influencing the outcome of the land deal. This discovery changed the focus of the investigation completely, shifting from a simple break-in to a complex case of corporate espionage and political corruption. Day, while having the skills to execute the heist, was merely a pawn in a much larger game.

The investigation revealed a conspiracy that reached into the highest echelons of power in Suva. Singh, however, knew that the evidence connecting Day to the larger conspiracy was circumstantial at best. There was no concrete evidence linking him directly to the land development deal, no proof he was acting on behalf of anyone else other than himself or his own motives.

The shadows of the past lingered, casting a long and complex pall over Suva's future. The case remained open, a testament to the enduring struggle between justice and the relentless pursuit of power.

Success and its Cost

He was a thief, a criminal, a man who'd traded his freedom for the chance to prove his love. The irony was sharp, bitter, and utterly inescapable. The ensuing days were a blur of anxiety and uncertainty. The successful operation bought him time, a precious commodity in his life, but it couldn't erase the moral ambiguity of his actions.

One evening sitting on the balcony of his room above the Roti Shop, the city lights twinkling like fallen stars, he felt the full weight of his dilemma. The thrill of the heist had faded, replaced by a profound sense of unease. His hands, usually nimble and quick, felt clumsy and heavy. The memories of the operation played on repeat in his mind – the cool steel of the lock, the hum of the servers, the silent urgency of his movements. Each memory was a painful reminder of the precarious line he walked, a constant dance on the edge of a knife.

Adelyn's love was his anchor, but the uncertainty of his future gnawed at him. Could he truly escape his past? Could he ever be the man she wanted him to be? The weight of his past sins pressed upon him, a heavy cloak he wore, its fabric woven from guilt and regret. He was a man of two worlds, a man caught between the life he had left behind and the life he desperately wanted to create. He needed to change, not just for Adelyn, but for himself. He knew he could not continue living this double life, this dangerous dance between love and lawlessness. He had to find a way to reconcile his past with his future and transform his skills into something constructive. It wouldn't lead to more heartache and betrayal.

The thought of his *thumbs*, his tools of the trade, his instruments of both creation and destruction haunted him. They were his curse and his blessing, his lifeline, these *dirty digits* were his downfall. The image of them, the delicate dexterity of them, and the precise movements they enabled were burned into his mind. He contemplated *the* drastic measure. The only way he knew to sever ties with his criminal past, a symbolic act of self-sacrifice, a testament to his resolve.

He had spent weeks preparing himself mentally, the task looming over him like a storm cloud. The decision was agonizing, a crucible of pain and self-doubt. In the silent sanctity of his room, a solemn, unbreakable vow took root, its gravity echoing deeply within him. He thought of Adelyn, her face, her love, her unwavering belief in him. That hope, that faith, fueled his resolve. The tools were simple, the method brutal, a harsh, *self-imposed amputation* that would leave him maimed, a physical sacrifice to match the emotional upheaval he'd endured.

The act itself was a blur, a mix of agony and a strange, twisted sense of liberation. The pain was excruciating, a searing wave of torment that nearly broke him. But through the pain, a sense of purpose appeared, the resolve to never again wield his skill in such a way. He would earn his place in Adelyn's world, not through the darkness of his past but through the honest labor of his future.

The days following the amputation were marked by immense physical pain and emotional turmoil. He was in agony, his body racked with pain, his spirit bruised. His love for Adelyn sustained him, her presence a beacon in his pain-filled world. Her care, her love, reminded him that she was worth the sacrifice.

The journey ahead would be long and arduous, a challenging path towards rehabilitation and redemption. The scars, both physical and emotional, were a testament to his past, a constant reminder of the price he'd paid for his love and the life he was working towards building.

He'd traded his ability to pick locks for the chance to build a future, a future he intended to cherish and protect. He'd faced his demons and emerged, wounded but not broken, ready to embrace a new life with the woman he loved. His past still lingered, but it no longer held him captive. He was free. Or so he hoped.

The Amputation

The rusty blade, scavenged from a discarded fishing net, felt cold against his skin. The kerosene lamp cast long, dancing shadows across the cracked concrete floor of his tiny room above the Roti Shop, illuminating the grim determination etched on Day's face. He'd chosen this place, this dingy space that held the scent of stale roti and his own sweat, as the stage for his desperate act. There was a perverse poetry to it, the act of self-mutilation occurring within the very confines of his life, a life he was so violently trying to sever. He'd practiced the precise angles, the necessary pressure, visualizing the cut, the pain, the inevitable crimson bloom. He'd imagined Adelyn's face, her horrified expression, the rapid, silent judgment of his actions. Yet, beneath the terror of it all, a strange calm had settled over him. This wasn't madness; it was a calculated sacrifice. A brutal offering at the altar of his love.

By the flickering kerosene lamp, he scorched the corroded blade. The gnarled, wooden haft, a brutal clamp, was secured between two wooden planks. His first cut unleashed a torment so profound, a searing inferno of pain, it threatened to obliterate him. His jaw clenched, bone-white knuckles gripping the crude table's splintered surface. He focused on Adelyn's image – her smile, the way her eyes crinkled at the corners when she laughed, the softness of her touch. These images fueled him, pushing back the tide of agony. Sweat beaded on his forehead, mingling with the grime of days spent hunched over locks and keys. He'd never been squeamish about blood, not from the countless scrapes and bruises acquired over years of petty crime, but this was different. This was self-inflicted, a deliberate tearing of his own flesh, a violent severing of his connection to his past.

With grim determination, he applied himself to the task. A second *digit* landed on the aged wood with a sickening, meaty impact. Excruciating pain, a brutal crescendo of torment, ravaged his body. His heart hammered a frantic rhythm against his ribs, a savage percussion going with his ordeal. But his resolve remained unshaken. No sound escaped his lips. He continued with chilling, methodical precision, each movement a testament to his steely will. He had watched enough medical dramas on the flickering television set downstairs to know the basic principles of amputation. The crude tools were inadequate, the method far from sterile, but he was driven by a desperate hope, a primal need to escape the life that had so cruelly bound him.

The blood flowed freely, a dark tide staining the floorboards. It pooled around his feet, a morbid reflection of the sacrifice he had made. He wrapped the wounds crudely with strips of his old shirt, the white cotton quickly turning crimson. The bandages felt heavy, suffocating. The throbbing was immense, but it was bearable, dulled by the overwhelming sense of relief. He had done it. He had broken the chains.

He looked down at his hands, or rather, the maimed remnants of his hands. They were no longer tools of his trade. The thumbs, those nimble, dexterous *dirty digits* that had opened so many locks, were gone, severed, sacrificed to a love as desperate as it was profound. This act wasn't solely about

Adelyn; it was a declaration to himself, a final, brutal renunciation of his criminal life.

With languid steps, he approached the window, the oppressive tropical night thick with the aroma of brine and rot. Suva, a constellation of glimmering lights and inky shadows, lay spread beneath the celestial tapestry. The Roti Shop, its inviting warmth a comforting island in the darkness, caught his eye. Beyond it, the distant hospital – Adelyn's sanctuary, where she ministered to the afflicted, oblivious to his desperate actions on her behalf – stood stark and silent.

A debilitating vertigo seized him, forcing him against the cool, unforgiving brick. He collapsed, his knees buckling beneath him, overcome by an exhaustion that gnawed at his very bones. Yet, amidst the profound weariness, a stark lucidity prevailed. He had paid a terrible cost, an exorbitant one. But for Adelyn, it was a sacrifice he embraced, even craved.

The kerosene lamp flickered, casting long, dancing shadows across the worn wooden floorboards of the Roti Shop's upper room. Adelyn sat beside Day, the air thick with the scent of antiseptic and something else, something primal and unsettling – the metallic tang of blood. His hands, bandaged crudely, lay still on the makeshift bed of blankets and old newspapers.

The silent screaming, broken only by the sporadic creaks of the aging building settling under the weight of the night. She hadn't screamed, hadn't fainted, hadn't even cried, not yet. Shock, a cold, clammy hand, had gripped her heart, leaving her breathless and strangely numb.

She had known, somehow, instinctively, that Day was capable

of great recklessness, of desperate acts born of love and a fierce desire for redemption. But this... this was beyond anything she could have imagined. The sight of his mutilated hands, the knowledge of the pain he must have endured, the sheer brutality of his self-inflicted wound, sent a wave of nausea crashing over her.

It was a perverse kind of love, this sacrificial offering. A love that transcended logic, that defied reason, that challenged the very fabric of their reality. He had offered himself, a piece of his very being, to appease some unseen deity, a god of their shared future. And she, caught in the crosscurrents of her emotions, felt a conflicting surge of relief and despair.

Relief, because he was alive. He had chosen life, a life with her, even if it meant this unspeakable mutilation. The terrifying prospect of losing him, of facing a future without his chaotic energy, his reckless charm, his undeniable presence had been a constant shadow. Now, that shadow, though distorted and terrifying, was still there, but lessened, diminished by the very act of his self-sacrifice. But the sadness... oh, the sadness was overwhelming. It was a crushing weight on her chest, a constant ache in her soul. The image of Day, his face pale and drawn, his eyes filled with a grim determination, would forever haunt her dreams. The thought of his pain, the agonizing process, the raw, brutal act of self-destruction – it was an image that burrowed into her mind, clinging to the edges of her consciousness. He had given up his life's work, his skill, a significant piece of his identity – all for her.

She reached out, her fingers hesitantly tracing the rough outline of the bandages. The fabric was stiff with dried blood, a testament to the enormity of his act. The touch sent a shiver down her spine, a mixture of revulsion and an almost overwhelming tenderness. She wanted to cry out, to rage against the injustice of it all, but the words caught in her throat, choked by the sheer enormity of his love. The next morning dawned with a pale, uncertain light. The pain was a constant companion, a dull ache that permeated every fiber of his being. He moved with difficulty, each movement a stark reminder of his drastic act. Yet he felt a sense of lightness he hadn't felt in years, a feeling unburdened from the constant pressure of criminal dealings.

Expertly, Adelyn crafted a simple yet comforting meal; a sparse offering of bread, paired with fragrant, freshly brewed tea, for him. Her deft fingers, honed by years of nursing, expertly dressed his wounded hands, the bandages and gave him a tetanus and penicillin shot, a testament to her compassionate skill. Day's mind raced, replaying the scene in his head, the act of self-mutilation, the raw agony, the finality of it all. He still couldn't believe he'd done it, but as he looked down at his hands, he found a strange sense of resolve. The scars, both physical and emotional, were deep, but they weren't wounds; they were badges of honor, testimonies to the depth of his love.

Later that day, Maddaar appeared at his door. He didn't speak much, simply handed Day a small, worn leather pouch. Inside, were herbs, carefully wrapped in dried pandanus leaves. "For the healing," Maddaar said, his voice raspy, his words few. "The body heals. The spirit too, if given the chance." He then turned and walked away, disappearing as quickly as he had

89

arrived, leaving Day with his unspoken wisdom.

Days bled into weeks. The first shock gradually gave way to a profound sense of grief, a quiet mourning for the loss of the man she had known, the skilled safecracker with nimble fingers, the man whose very essence was tied to his ability to manipulate locks and evade the law. That man was gone, replaced by a shadow of his former self, a man struggling to adapt to a world where his once-prized skill was now a crippling disability.

The Roti Shop, once a familiar backdrop to their story, now felt sterile, devoid of the vibrant energy that had always been a part of Day's presence. The aroma of freshly cooked rotis and rare spices, a heady perfume masking a profound grief, hung heavy in the atmosphere. Even the lively chatter of the patrons felt muted, almost respectful of the silent suffering unfolding above.

Adelyn spent her days at the hospital, her work a dull routine offering a much-needed distraction. The familiar faces, the comforting rhythm of the hospital's routines, provided a temporary reprieve from the turmoil that raged within her. But the evenings were the hardest. She would climb the rickety stairs to the room above the Roti Shop, each step a reminder of the sacrifice Day had made. She helped him, patiently, with the arduous tasks of daily life. Simple things, once effortless, now needed immense patience and concentration. Buttoning his shirt, tying his shoelaces, eating, even holding a cup of tea – everything became a challenge. Yet, she noticed a strange resilience in him, a determined spirit that mirrored her own. She spent hours reading to him, her voice a soothing balm against the gnawing pain that still plagued him. They spoke little, their conversation limited to the necessities, but their silence held a depth of understanding that transcended words. His eyes, dark and intense, held a flicker of gratitude, a glimmer of hope. One evening, as she sat beside him, his hand resting lightly in hers, he spoke. His voice was weak, barely a whisper, yet it held an unshakable resolve. "I did it for us," he said, his gaze unwavering.

Days turned into weeks. The pain gradually subsided, replaced by the dull ache of healing wounds. The pungent aroma of the ginger, turmeric, and lemongrass filled the air, a fragrant counterpoint to the lingering scent of blood. Adelyn visited him regularly, her visits a silent acknowledgment of his extraordinary sacrifice. Their conversations were strained, marked by an awkward silence, a mutual understanding of the gravity of his act.

Adelyn was torn. She loved Day, a love that had weathered countless storms, but the amputation had taken a toll on their relationship. The image of his wounded hands, the raw, visceral act of self-harm, haunted her waking hours. She battled with feelings of fear, of anger, of profound sadness. She questioned his sanity, his judgment, the very nature of their bond. But beneath all this turmoil, a fragile spark of hope remained. A flicker of faith in the man who had sacrificed so much for her.

One evening, under the soft glow of the setting sun, Adelyn sat beside Day in his small room. She held his hands, his bandaged hands, feeling the phantom weight of his missing thumbs. "Day," she began, her voice hesitant, "I...I don't understand." Day looked at her, his eyes reflecting the golden hues of the fading light. "I know," he replied softly, "It was…it was a drastic act. But I had to show you, show everyone, that I was serious about changing. That I was ready to leave that life behind, for good." "But what about you?" Adelyn whispered. "What kind of life can you have without your thumbs?" He smiled, a sad yet determined smile. "A different life, Adelyn. A better life. A life with you."

The silence that followed was not filled with accusations or doubt, but with a shared understanding of the depth of their love, the profound sacrifice Day had made, and the long, difficult road they would walk together, hand in hand. He had given up his tools, his identity, a part of himself; yet he gained something far more valuable: a chance at a future, free from the shadows of the past, a future built on the foundations of love and sacrifice.

The path ahead was unclear, but he had Adelyn's hand in his, and that was enough. His amputation was an end, but also a beginning, a testament to a love that defied logic, reason, and the very laws that governed his world. The city of Suva, with its vibrant life and its hidden darkness, would see the slow, painful, yet ultimately hopeful journey of a man who traded his thumbs for a future.

Adelyn squeezed his hand, the gesture conveying more than words could ever express. His sacrifice wasn't just an act of love, it was a testament to his commitment to a future they would build together, brick by brick, despite the obstacles.

She learned to adapt, to help him in ways she never thought

possible. She learned patience, understanding, and a deeper appreciation for his strength. The once-feared shadows of his past, now softened by the bright light of his sacrifice, illuminated not only his journey but also her own growth and evolution. The frenetic city of Suva, with all its vibrant energy and shadowy secrets, bore witness to the metamorphosis of their love, a love reborn from ashes, tempered by pain, but ultimately, stronger than ever before.

She often found herself staring out the window, at the vibrant life unfolding below, the bustling streets of Suva. The sounds of distant laughter and the rhythm of life in the city below now brought a sense of peace, rather than the anxious anticipation that had been her constant companion. The constant fear for Day's safety, the gnawing worry about his criminal activities, had been replaced by a quiet hope, a profound trust, and the determined acceptance of their future. The future wasn't certain, it never was, and they knew it. Yet, in the face of adversity, they had found something far stronger than fear – they had found each other, their love assessed and refined, appeared triumphant and more profoundly connected than ever before.

The city lights twinkled like a million tiny stars against the vast, velvety sky, mirroring the infinite possibilities of their future. Adelyn knew that the scars, both visible and invisible, would remain, but they would be a testament to their love, a reminder of the sacrifices made, the battles fought, and the unwavering commitment to building a life together, defying all odds. The transformation wasn't just Day's; it was their shared journey, a testament to the resilience of the human spirit, the enduring power of love, and the unwavering hope that bloomed even in the darkest corners of their lives. The future was uncertain, yes, but it was theirs, forged in the crucible of pain, love, and sacrifice. And that, she realized, was enough. More than enough.

Maddaar's Revelation

The chipped paint of Maddaar's veranda flaked onto the worn wooden floorboards, mirroring the decay that seemed to cling to the old man himself. He sat hunched, a skeletal figure draped in a faded floral shirt, his eyes, the colour of faded sapphires, fixed on the turbulent sea beyond. The air hung heavy with the scent of salt and decaying hibiscus, a fitting aroma for this den of secrets. Day, restless and anxious, shifted on the rickety chair opposite him. The silence stretched, punctuated only by the rhythmic crash of waves against the shore. Ravinesh Singh's investigation had left Day with a gnawing unease, a feeling of being watched, even though the detective had been strangely lenient.

Finally, Maddaar spoke, his voice a low rasp, like dry leaves skittering across pavement. "You think they've let you off easy, Day Marshall? The police… they're blind sometimes, but not always. They see what they want to see." He paused, taking a slow, deliberate drag from a hand-rolled cigarette. The smoke curled around his face, obscuring his expression.

"They saw a thief who cut off his own hands. A man desperate for redemption. But they didn't see the boy."

Day flinched. The "boy" – a forgotten part of himself, buried under years of petty crimes and larger schemes. He hadn't thought about that boy in years, the boy who'd once dreamed of becoming a carpenter, his hands shaping wood into intricate designs.

95

"What about the boy, Maddaar?" Day's voice was barely a whisper, the question hanging in the air between them, thick with unspoken fears and regrets. Maddaar chuckled, a dry, crackling sound. "The boy… he was stolen from his family. Taken away. Not just his life, but his very identity."

The words hit Day like a physical blow. He knew nothing of his origins, his past a blank canvas, painted only with the grim colours of the streets and the harsh reality of survival. He had always assumed his parents had simply abandoned him; he'd created that narrative to shield himself from the deeper pain of not knowing. "Stolen?" Day repeated, his voice catching in his throat. "By whom?" "The same hands that dealt your family a cruel blow, Day. The same hands that plunged them into debt and despair," Maddaar responded, his gaze unwavering. "The hands that created you, the thief, were the same hands that stole your innocence."

Maddaar's disclosure cast a suffocating shadow over the oppressive humidity. A bitter land feud, a tangled conspiracy of bribery and treachery involving prominent landowners and high-ranking officials, formed the dark heart of his story. His family, it happened, had owned a sizable part of the very land upon which the hospital now stood – a prize relentlessly coveted by influential figures who, through calculated bullying and legal deception, systematically stripped them of their inheritance. Unable to discharge the trumped-up debts levied against them, his grandparents were reduced to dire poverty, their lives shattered beyond repair.

Maddaar didn't explicitly say it, but Day understood. The theft of his family's land had been the true theft – the theft of his childhood, his identity, his future. The years he spent on the streets, learning the grim trade of safecracking, weren't simply a consequence of circumstance; they were a desperate attempt to reclaim what had been stolen from him– his livelihood, his dignity, his sense of belonging.

The theft hadn't been a single act, Maddaar explained. It had been a slow, insidious process, woven into the fabric of the Fijian judicial system, a system that often favored the powerful and left the vulnerable exposed. His family's case was just one amongst many, lost in the bureaucratic labyrinth, a testament to the systemic corruption that plagued the island nation.

Maddaar's revelations peeled back layers of Day's life, exposing a raw, wounded core. The safecracking hadn't been about the thrill of the heist, or the money, as Day had always told himself. It was a form of rebellion, a desperate act of defiance against a system that had robbed him of everything. Each lock he picked was a symbolic act of reclaiming his stolen past, a defiant middle finger to the forces that had driven him to the fringes of society.

The old man continued, his voice growing stronger, imbued with a fierce determination. "They took your land, Day, but they couldn't take your spirit. They couldn't take your skill. They thought they could break you, but you survived."

Day listened, his heart pounding against his ribs, a mixture of anger and sorrow swirling within him. The pieces of the puzzle were finally falling into place, revealing a hidden narrative that cast a new light on his actions. He was not merely a thief; he was a survivor, a victim of a larger, more insidious crime.

The obliteration of those medical files was far more sinister than simple historical erasure; it was a calculated attempt to conceal a vast conspiracy extending far beyond mere property disputes. This deliberate act ensured the silenced cries of the victims, including Day's family, would forever echo unheard in the annals of history. His pulse thundered in his ears—was it truly so? Could Adelyn, Adelyn, have known? The horrifying realization struck him like a blow.

Adelyn…Adelyn knew? Adelyn knew!

The conversation stretched into the night, the old man revealing snippets of information that painted a stark picture of corruption within the Suva elite. He spoke of silenced whistleblowers, shady deals, and manipulated legal processes; a system rigged to protect the powerful, leaving the vulnerable to fend for themselves. He spoke of corruption, a malignant web woven throughout the island, ensnared politicians, entrepreneurs, and even judicial figures in its insidious grasp.

Day, armed with this newfound knowledge, felt a surge of anger and a renewed sense of purpose. His amputation hadn't ended his fight; it had merely redefined. "You knew," he growled, his voice thick with suspicion, "about the vile corruption entwining my family's land with the hospital's depraved transactions!"

The stealing of those medical records was far more than a simple act of historical revisionism; it was a desperate, ruthless attempt to bury a vast, malignant conspiracy that dwarfed any mere property squabble. Could this be true? The galling bitterness of betrayal still coated his tongue, yet Adelyn, a vision in pristine white, stood beside him, a shocking, unexpected ally. This wasn't a mere struggle over an antiquated inheritance; it was a fight for his family's very spirit, a battle for their survival. And Adelyn—Adelyn, with her unnerving composure and formidable determination—was his improbable, radiant instrument of defiance. Her enigmatic motivations, cloaked in mystery, hinted at a past as treacherous and intricate as the web of deceit they were dismantling. *She* engineered this. For *him*. For *his family*. The crushing weight of her sacrifice, the terrifying size of her commitment, threatened to overwhelm him.

Adelyn's Acceptance

Assigned an office project concerning the Native Land Trust Board's contentious dispute with CWM Hospitals' land entitlements, Adelyn unearthed a pivotal name: Marshall. This surname, her research revealed, was Day's maternal ancestry – a lineage of mixed European heritage. His Fijian father's family had historically held a substantial part of the land upon which the *new wing of the hospital* now stood. Deep within the documents, a shocking tale of land-grabbing unfolded – a web of vicious intrigue and corrupt dealings among government officials. Forged documents and outright deception had irrevocably shattered the lives of Day's grandparents, leaving a legacy of profound injustice.

Confession spilled from her lips: a meticulously crafted scheme to incite him, to galvanize his dormant spirit into reclaiming his ancestral heritage. She revealed how, amidst the drudgery of her professional tasks, she unearthed the irrefutable proof of his family's land rights. This revelation, she intended to share with him on the very night of his harrowing self-mutilation.

She hadn't rushed to judgment, hadn't thrown accusations or uttered recriminations. Instead, she'd listened, absorbing the weight of his words, the burden of his past. She saw the boy he once was, trapped in a cycle of poverty and desperation, forced to make choices that chipped away at his soul. She saw the man he was now, scarred but striving, desperate to break free from the shadows that had haunted him for so long.

The image of his bloodied hands, the raw stumps where his thumbs once were, flashed vividly in her mind. The sight had been horrifying, a visceral reminder of the lengths he'd gone to for her, for a future free from the clutches of the underworld. It was a love so fierce, so consuming, that it bordered on madness, a love that had driven him to such drastic measures.

And yet, within that madness, she saw a profound clarity, a desperate yearning for redemption. His self-sacrifice wasn't a sign of weakness; it was an act of profound strength, a testament to the depths of his remorse and his unwavering commitment to their future.

The scent of the sea air, sharp and clean, helped to clear the fog in her mind. The relentless rhythm of the waves was a soothing balm, washing away the residue of her anger and confusion. The sun dipped below the horizon, painting the sky in hues of fiery orange and deep violet. The light reflected on the water, creating a mesmerizing spectacle of shimmering colours. Adelyn stood there, bathed in the fading light, a renewed sense of purpose filling her. She would be his anchor, his unwavering support in the turbulent waters of their lives. She would help him navigate the treacherous currents of his past, guiding him towards a future where his actions were defined not by the shadows he'd escaped, but by the light of their love.

She understood now. She understood the choices he'd made, the circumstances that had molded him, the weight of his past that he carried with him like a second skin. It wasn't an excuse for his actions, but it was an explanation, a heartbreaking glimpse into the soul of the man she loved.

The weight of that realization settled upon her, heavy and profound. This wasn't just about Day's past; it was about their future, a future that they would have to forge together, brick by painstaking brick. It would be a future filled with challenges, with hurdles that would evaluate the strength of their bond. But she was ready. She was ready to face them together, side by side.

She thought of Ravinesh Singh, the detective, and his ambiguous words. The implication of a larger conspiracy, a network of corruption that reached into the highest echelons of Suva's society, was chilling. Day's involvement, however misguided, had placed him squarely in the crosshairs of powerful and ruthless individuals. His self-mutilation was not just a desperate attempt to escape his criminal past; it was a calculated move to remove himself from their reach, to sever the ties that bound him to that dangerous world.

The next morning, Adelyn arrived at the Roti Shop, the aroma of curried meat pie filling the air. Day was already awake, his gaze fixed on the steaming cup of tea in his hands. His face, though still etched with the weariness of his ordeal, held a flicker of hope. The absence of his thumbs was stark, a painful reminder of his sacrifice, but his eyes held a newfound clarity, a steely resolve that resonated deep within Adelyn.

She approached him cautiously, her heart pounding in her chest. The silence between them was thick with unspoken emotions, a testament to the unspoken understanding that had grown between them. She sat down opposite him, her hand reaching across the table, her fingers gently brushing his. His touch was hesitant at first, then firm and reassuring.

"I understand," she whispered, her voice thick with emotion. "I understand everything."

He looked up at her, his eyes filled with a mixture of relief and gratitude. "You do?" he asked, his voice barely a breath.

"Yes," she replied, her gaze unwavering. "I see the boy you were, the man you are, and the man you are becoming. And I love you, Day. With all my heart."

His eyes welled up, tears streaming down his face. He reached for her hand, his grip tight and unwavering. "I'm so sorry, Adelyn. I've put you through hell."

"It's okay," she said softly, stroking his hand. "We'll face it together. We'll rebuild our lives together. We'll create a future that is worthy of our love."

The following weeks were a blur of activity. Adelyn helped Day navigate the bureaucratic maze of his rehabilitation, ensuring he received the best possible care. She visited him daily at the physiotherapy clinic, her presence a constant source of support and encouragement. She watched as he slowly regained his strength, his determination unwavering.

She saw the frustration in his eyes, the yearning for independence, but also the quiet acceptance of his new reality. He was learning to adapt, to adjust to a life without his thumbs. It was a slow, arduous process, but he persisted, his resilience fueled by his love for Adelyn and his unwavering desire to build a better future. He learned to use adaptive tools, to master new techniques that allowed him to perform tasks that once seemed impossible. He was learning to live with his past, to integrate it into his present, to transform it into a source of strength.

Adelyn also took steps to address her own past traumas, the unresolved issues that had contributed to her first skepticism and frustration with Day. She sought therapy, allowing herself to confront her own insecurities and vulnerabilities. She began to understand the roots of her anger and resentment, the ways in which her own past had shaped her feelings of Day's actions.

Their relationship deepened during this period; their bond strengthened by the shared experiences of overcoming adversity. They learned to communicate more effectively, to express their needs and emotions openly and honestly. They found solace in each other's presence, in the simple act of sharing a meal, a quiet moment of reflection, a shared laugh. They weren't just a couple; they were a team, a unit working together to overcome the challenges life threw their way.

Confronting the Past

The humid Suva air hung heavy as Day sat on the worn wooden stool in Maddaar's veranda, the rhythmic chirping of crickets a stark contrast to the turmoil within him. He stared out at the star-dusted sky, the immensity of the cosmos mirroring the vastness of his own regret. Adelyn's words, her choked sobs, her quiet acceptance mingled with a hesitant hope, echoed in his ears. He had shown her the raw, bleeding stumps where his thumbs used to be, a grotesque testament to his desperate bid for redemption. He'd expected revulsion, disgust, perhaps even a final, heartbreaking rejection. Instead, he found something deeper, something that ignited a flicker of hope in the desolate landscape of his soul.

His mind drifted to a bleak childhood; a cramped, impoverished shack shared with siblings whose fates now remained unknown. He had shown a shocking neglect, never trying to find them; yet a flicker of resolve ignited – perhaps he would search for them now. The persistent pangs of hunger, the threadbare garments, the crushing sense of inferiority – these were the harsh realities that had blossomed into the cynical despair of his adulthood. He remembered his father, a man broken by circumstance, his hands calloused from years of backbreaking labor, his spirit crushed by unrelenting poverty. He hadn't been a criminal, not in the way Day had become, but he had been a victim, a casualty of a system that offered little in the way of opportunity or hope. Day's path had been a twisted, desperate attempt to escape that legacy, a misguided rebellion against a fate he felt destined to inherit.

His early forays into petty theft had been fueled by a desperate need to survive, to provide for his family in a way his father couldn't. The thrill, the adrenaline rush of outsmarting the authorities, had initially masked the underlying pain and despair. But as time went on, the thrill became less potent, the consequences more severe. The cycle of crime, incarceration, and release had become a suffocating vortex, pulling him further and further into the darkness. Each arrest, each court appearance, had been a stark reminder of his failures, his inability to break free from the grip of his past. He had even felt a perverse sense of comfort in the familiarity of the prison walls, a dark irony that he only utterly understood now.

One evening, as the sun dipped below the horizon, painting the sky in hues of fiery orange and deep purple, Adelyn turned to Day, her eyes reflecting the breathtaking spectacle. "I never thought I'd see this day," she whispered, her voice thick with emotion. "I never thought you could find your way back to the light." Day took her hand, his touch gentle, his eyes filled with a deep, abiding love. "I couldn't have done it without you," he said, his voice raw with emotion. "You gave me the strength I didn't know I had. You gave me a reason to fight."

Their silence was punctuated only by the gentle sounds of the evening – the soft lapping of waves against the shore, the chirping of crickets, the distant hum of the city. It was a silence filled with unspoken words, a testament to the unspoken understanding that bound them together, stronger than any lock, more precious than any treasure. The fragility of their peace was clear, a delicate balance easily disrupted, but it was a peace they would fiercely protect, a peace they were ready to fight for.

He thought of his past heists, the meticulous planning, the adrenaline-pumping execution, the satisfaction of the perfect score. Each successful job had been a temporary victory, a fleeting moment of triumph in a life characterized by defeat. But each victory had been followed by a heavier consequence, a longer sentence, a deeper sense of isolation.

The faces of his victims flickered through his mind, each one a silent accusation, a weight on his conscience he could no longer ignore. He remembered the elderly woman "anda nani" (egg seller) whose life savings he'd stolen, the fear in her eyes, the tremor in her voice. He had justified it then, rationalized it as unavoidable, a means to an end. Now, the memory was a searing brand on his soul, a constant reminder of the harm he had caused. He could no longer hide from the gravity of his actions, could no longer run from the consequences. The severed thumbs were a physical manifestation of his resolve, a brutal act of self-punishment, but more importantly, a symbolic severing of his past life.

The scent of frangipani and salt drifted in on the night breeze, a poignant reminder of the beauty of Fiji, the land he had betrayed with his actions. He thought of Adelyn, her unwavering love a beacon in the darkness. Her love had not been blind; she had seen his darkest deeds, yet she had chosen to remain, to offer forgiveness and hope where he had only found despair.

The hospital, once a symbol of their separation, now stood for a shared victory. Adelyn's work brought her a sense of purpose, while Day's newfound carpentry skills earned him a humble but respectable livelihood, supporting them as a couple. They celebrated small milestones – a completed piece of furniture, a smoothly run hospital shift, a shared meal under the star-dusted sky. They were building a life together, slow and steady, one precious moment at a time.

He knew that rebuilding his life would be an uphill battle, but he wasn't alone in this struggle. He had Adelyn, Maddaar, and the quiet support of the small community that had tolerated his past. They stood for a chance, a fragile chance, to reclaim his life, to prove that even someone with his history could find *redemption*. The Roti Shop, once a symbol of his precarious existence, could now become a symbol of his hard-earned success.

The scars of his past were etched into his very being, both physical and emotional. But they would not define him. They would serve as a constant reminder of the darkness he'd escaped, the darkness he would never return to. He was finally ready to confront the light, even if it was a long and arduous journey. He would walk that path with Adelyn by his side, their love a beacon guiding them towards a future free from the shadows that had haunted them for so long. The path to redemption was long and arduous, but for the first time in a long time, Day felt a glimmer of hope, a sense of genuine peace. He was ready. He had to be. For Adelyn. For himself. For the future they were finally ready to build together, a future where the past was a lesson, not a life sentence.

The Roti Shop's Future

From the Roti Shop's core, the irresistible fragrance of savory samosas and crispy fritters wafted, a comforting balm to the spirit, intrinsically woven into the very fabric of the day. The small diner, nestled amongst the vibrant chaos of Suva, had always been more than just a place of business; it was a sanctuary, a refuge, a testament to all the customers.

Weary from years of toil, Papa Ram and Mama Sita, longed for the tranquil embrace of their native Levuka, nestled on the idyllic Vanua Levu Island. Retirement beckoned, a well-deserved respite. Reluctant to entrust their beloved Roti Shop to any unworthy hands, they extended a generous offer of ownership to Day and Adelyn. Financial expediency held no sway; their priority lay in ensuring a seamless transition of their culinary legacy.

Day leaned against the counter, the smooth, cool surface a welcome contrast to the phantom ache in his missing thumbs. The shop, once a backdrop to his clandestine activities, now held the promise of a legitimate livelihood, a future built on honest sweat and unwavering love. Adelyn, her presence a constant source of calm amidst the whirlwind of his life, hummed softly as she organized the spice rack. The gentle rhythm of her movements, the way her brow furrowed in concentration as she meticulously arranged the bottles of garam masala and other spices, grounded Day in the present. He watched her, a silent observer, his heart swelling with a love that transcended the trials and tribulations they had endured.

The Roti Shop, once a symbol of his duality—the place where he lived above, hidden from the scrutiny of the law while simultaneously serving as a cover for his activities—was now a symbol of their unity, their shared future. They adapted. Day, with his resourceful nature intact despite the loss of his thumbs, learned to adapt his methods. He taught himself to use specialized tools to prepare the dough, his movements deliberate, precise. The loss of his dexterity only sharpened his focus, his determination burning brighter than ever. He discovered a surprising talent for creating intricate roti designs, each one a testament to his resilience and a symbol of his new beginning.

He started to experiment with new recipes, infusing flavors inspired by his Fijian heritage. He'd always had a natural aptitude for cooking, but now, it was more than just a skill; it was a form of self-expression, a way of channeling his energy and emotions into something positive and constructive. He began sourcing ingredients locally, forging connections with farmers and suppliers, building relationships that extended beyond mere business transactions.

Word spread. The Roti Shop, once a quiet haven, became a bustling hub, a place where people came not just for the delicious food, but also for the warmth and welcoming atmosphere Day and Adelyn cultivated. The locals, charmed by their dedication and the unique flavor of their rotis, became loyal customers, their patronage a testament to Day's transformation. Golden sunlight flooded the once dim lit Roti Shop, painting the lush foliage and sparkling panes in a radiant glow. Day and Adelyn's revitalization imbued the space with a palpable vitality, a radiant warmth that hinted at flourishing life within. No longer just a roti vendor, the shop had evolved into a dynamic community haven where a tapestry of lives intertwined, and friendships blossomed. Even Maddaar, the enigmatic recluse, became a regular, his silent presence a comforting anomaly in the vibrant atmosphere.

The Roti Shop became a symbol of their new life—a life built on the foundations of love, forgiveness, and a shared commitment to build something meaningful together. Day's criminal past didn't disappear, but it faded into the background, overshadowed by the vibrant tapestry of their present and future. The scars remained—both physical and emotional—but they were badges of honor, reminders of their resilience and the strength of their love.

The sunrise over Suva was indeed a symbol of their hope, a daily affirmation of their shared journey, a quiet promise of a future bathed in the warmth of their enduring love. Their love story, once a dark tale woven in shadows and secrets, was now a radiant sunrise, a testament to their triumphant new beginning, forever etched in the heart of Suva, in the aroma of the Roti Shop.

Hope for the Future

The rhythmic pulse of the city, usually a jarring counterpoint to the quiet intimacy of their balcony, now seemed to hum a song of optimism. The sounds – the distant rumble of buses, the chatter of vendors setting up their stalls at the Suva Market, the cries of gulls circling overhead – were the soundtrack to their new beginning. Day watched Adelyn, the sunrise catching the faintest freckles dusting her nose. Her smile, radiant and genuine, was the most beautiful thing he'd ever seen, eclipsing even the breathtaking panorama of Suva harbour spread before them. Gone was the haunted look in her eyes, the constant shadow of worry that had clung to her since his last arrest. In its place was a quiet confidence, a sense of peace that mirrored his own.

He traced the delicate curve of her jawline, his fingers brushing lightly against her skin. The absence of his own thumbs, a sacrifice made for a future they both craved, felt less like a loss and more like a symbolic shedding of his old self. The raw, throbbing pain of the amputation was a distant memory, dulled by the potent analgesic of their shared hope. The phantom sensation of his thumbs, a constant reminder of his past, now served as a powerful symbol of his commitment, a tangible manifestation of his transformation. He had given up his skill, his curse, his livelihood – his very identity as Day Marshall, the safecracker – for her. And in doing so, he had found something far more valuable: a future with Adelyn.

112

The aroma of freshly brewed coffee, wafting from the Roti Shop below, mingled with the sweet scent of frangipani blossoms drifting on the morning breeze. It was a scent he associated with Adelyn, with her gentle spirit, her unwavering strength. It was the scent of home. The Roti Shop, once a refuge, a symbol of his precarious existence, now felt like a foundation, a solid base from which to build their life together. He looked down at the bustling activity below, a microcosm of Suva's vibrant life, a life he was now fully prepared to take part in, to contribute to, not as an outsider looking in, but as an active and honest member of his community.

August blazed, a colossal cruise liner dominating Suva's wharf. A vibrant throng of tourists, clad in sandals, sun hats, and minimal attire, swarmed the area, negotiating fiercely with vendors over intricately carved wood and authentic Fijian fabrics. The electrifying energy of Hibiscus Festival week crackled in the air.

Fiji's Hibiscus Festival, an annual spectacle, a vibrant testament to the nation's rich cultural tapestry. Traditional artistry unfolding through captivating performances, exquisite art exhibitions, and flamboyant processions, highlighting the splendor of Fijian heritage. The festival pulsates with the rhythm of Indigenous music and dance, a captivating display of grace and skill, complemented by an array of culinary masterpieces. It's a harmonious celebration, a testament to the unity of Fiji's diverse communities, bound together by a shared appreciation for nature's bounty.

Food vendors tantalize the senses with an enticing array of traditional Fijian fare. Savory dishes like *palusami,* taro leaves delicately baked in creamy coconut milk, and the refreshing *kokoda*, a zesty fish ceviche, are just a glimpse of the gastronomic delights on offer. The festival proudly emphasizes locally sourced ingredients and time-honored cooking methods, such as the *lovo,* an earth oven reflecting the profound connection between Fijian culture and its natural environment. Fiji's vibrant Indian community is richly represented at this festival, a culinary celebration highlighting the nation's diverse gastronomic heritage. A captivating array of authentic *Gujarati* and *South Indian* dishes and street foods promises an unforgettable feast for the senses. Day and Adelyn were proudly unveiling the Roti Shop's exciting new menu at their captivating booth, offering a tantalizing exploration of flavor.

He imagined the future, a future painted in vivid colours, rich and warm like the Fijian sun. They would expand the Roti Shop. He could picture Adelyn, radiating her usual calm efficiency, managing the accounts, her smile a beacon of welcome for their customers. He would be there to help, not with his nimble fingers picking locks, but with his hands, strong and capable, now free from the shackles of his criminal past, preparing food, cleaning, greeting customers, contributing to the lively atmosphere of the place. He saw them attending community events, taking part in community feasts, truly becoming part of the fabric of Suva.

Their relationship wouldn't be without its challenges. He knew that. The scars of the past wouldn't disappear overnight, but they could be healed. The trust that Adelyn had given him, after the betrayal and heartache, was something sacred, something he would cherish and protect more than anything else. He would prove to her, to everyone, that he was capable of change. He would show them that redemption was possible, even for a man like him, even for a safecracker who once believed his hands were only destined for illegal pursuits.

He thought about the external hard drive brimming with incriminating evidence. They had sought the counsel of prominent legal eagles with Maddaar's financial help. Their mission: to dismantle the entrenched corruption within Suva's power structure – a cabal of politicians and a compromised judiciary that had brutally silenced whistleblowers and cynically manipulated the legal framework.

Fueled by righteous distress over the wrongful appropriation of their ancestral lands, Day and Adelyn waged a tireless campaign for resolve the issue. They argued that the courts, through their collaboration with the hospital's construction, had enabled this appalling injustice. Their demand was for significant monetary amends to compensate for the profound and lasting harm inflicted upon them. The path ahead promised to be arduous and protracted, yet their resolve would remain unshaken.

He thought of Maddaar, the enigmatic recluse who had, in his own cryptic way, provided a sort of mentorship, a silent witness to Day's transformation. Maddaar's quiet wisdom, his understanding of the complexities of human nature, had provided a much-needed perspective, a reminder that even those who stumble can find their way back to the light. His unexpected, and deeply appreciated, intervention securing premier legal representation for the land dispute proved invaluable. He hoped to find Maddaar someday and express his gratitude, perhaps even share in a quiet moment of reflection over a bowl of kava.

Adelyn stirred, her eyes slowly fluttering open. She smiled, a gentle, sleepy smile that melted away any lingering anxieties. "The sun's up," she murmured, her voice still thick with sleep. "And so is our future," Day replied, his voice husky with emotion. He pulled her closer, enveloping her in a warm embrace, the scent of her perfume – a blend of coconut and jasmine – a comforting reminder of the journey they'd shared.

The sun climbed higher, painting the sky in a breathtaking display of colour. The bustling sounds of Suva were a symphony of hope, a promise of a bright and beautiful future. The rhythmic crash of waves against the seawall was no longer a lullaby, but a celebration – a celebration of their love, their redemption, and their unwavering belief in the possibility of a second chance. It was a sunrise over Suva, a sunrise that heralded a new dawn, a dawn filled with the promise of a future as bright and limitless as the ocean stretching before them.

He thought of the children they might have one day, children who would grow up in the warm embrace of a loving family, children who would never have to experience the darkness and despair that had once consumed him. He imagined them playing on the beach, their laughter echoing across the turquoise waters, their happiness a radiant testament to the love that had brought him and Adelyn together.

The future was unwritten, a canvas waiting to be filled with the vibrant colours of their shared dreams. And with every sunrise over Suva, they would paint their own masterpiece, a masterpiece of love, redemption, and hope. A masterpiece that would be whispered on the gentle sea breeze, a story that would resonate with the enduring spirit of Suva, Fiji, a story that would inspire others to believe in the possibility of second chances and the transformative power of unwavering love.

Acknowledgments

My formative years in Suva, Fiji, my birthplace, were indelibly shaped by its people, their generosity profoundly influencing my understanding of Fijian culture. The city's pulsating rhythm, the cacophony of its markets, and the tranquil intimacy of its quaint shops—these experiences wove themselves into the very fabric of my being. The principal characters, Day and Adelyn, bear the names of my beloved, deceased parents—Uday Narayan and my mother's baptismal name, Adelyn, a poignant tribute to their enduring legacy. My childhood years are indelibly etched with the vibrant personas of my youth. School friends, their joyous peals still ringing in my ears, were interwoven with the comforting presence of neighbours who became trusted companions. And at the heart of it all, my family, the unwavering foundation upon which my early life was built.

This narrative, however, is a fabrication, entirely separate from reality, bearing no resemblance to any person or locale. The names employed are drawn from the wellspring of my childhood memories and the evocative landscape of my homeland.

Finally, I want to express my gratitude to my editor, Amazon Classic Publishers whose insightful feedback and guidance helped me shape this story into its final form. Your ability and dedication significantly improved the manuscript, and I am deeply appreciative of your contributions.

www.ingramcontent.com/pod-product-compliance
Lightning Source LLC
Chambersburg PA
CBHW050456110726
47899CB00003B/959